FOREVER GOALS

A RIXON HIGH EPILOGUE

L A COTTON

Published by Delesty Books

FOREVER GOALS
Copyright © L. A. Cotton 2023
All rights reserved.

This book is a work of fiction. Names, characters, places, and events are the product of the author's imagination or used in a fictitious manner. Any resemblance to actual persons or events is purely coincidental.

No part of this book may be reproduced or used in any manner without the written permission of the publisher, except by a reviewer who may quote brief passages for review purposes only.

Edited and Proofread by Sisters Get Lit.erary Author Services

RIXON HIGH

Blurred Lines
A Rixon High Prequel Story

Off-Limits
A Rixon High Story

Tragic Lies
A Rixon High Story

Reckless Games
A Rixon High Novella

Ruined Hopes
A Rixon High Story

Broken Ties

RIXON HIGH

A Rixon High Story

Missed Notes
A Rixon High Story

Forever Goals
A Rixon High Epilogue

Play Hard... Fight Hard... Love Hard.
To all my Rixon fans, this one's for you!

CHAPTER ONE

KAIDEN

"CONGRATULATIONS, SON." Jason pulled me in for a one-armed hug, clapping me on the back. "I'm real damn proud of you, kid."

"Thanks." I stepped back, running a hand down my face.

"You good?" He studied me, and I desperately tried to school my expression.

"Y-yeah. All good, sir. But I was hoping—"

"There you are. My boy." Mom swept me into her arms. "Gosh, I'm so proud of you."

"Thanks, Mom."

"Where's Lily? I wanted to get a picture of the two of you."

"I'm not sure." It had been kind of crazy since we

spilled out of the graduation ceremony to the crowd of friends and family all wanting to celebrate with us, and I'd lost her in the chaos.

"Can you see her?" I asked Jason and Felicity as they scanned the crowd for their daughter.

"Nope. But I'm sure she's around here... Oh. There she is." Felicity's expression softened as we watched Lily approach with Poppy and Aaron in tow.

"Kaiden, my man," Aaron held out his hand. "Looking good Mr. NFL Hotshot."

"Babe," Poppy chided. "We talked about this, remember?"

"Come on, Poppystar. Kaiden was drafted to one of the best teams in the country, you can't expect me not to—"

"Aaron." Lily shook her head, nestling herself to my side. "Hey." She gazed up at me, and I fucking hated the glint of uncertainty there.

The last few months should have been the best of my life after I'd been drafted to one of the top teams in the NFL. But things between me and Lily were strained. My contract with the Kansas Wild would have me move a thousand miles across the country next week for rookie training camp. Then me and Lily planned to spend some time in Kansas, apartment hunting so that we'd be ready for her to join me for the start of the season.

With her cousin Avery getting married in a few weeks, and Peyton seven months pregnant, she wanted to spend some time in Rixon with them.

It made sense for me to make the move alone at first. I needed to gel with the team and fight for my place on the roster. But I didn't relish the idea of being apart from Lily. Not after four years of having her so close.

"Hey." I dropped a kiss on her head, wondering how I was supposed to leave her behind in less than a week.

I kept telling myself it was temporary, that it would all be worth it, but I couldn't ignore the seed of doubt taking root in my chest.

"I can't believe college is over," Poppy said, breaking the tension a little. "You did it, Lilster."

"That's it now, out in the big wide world." Aaron grinned. "At least you won't have to worry about finding a job especially since you're with Mr. Hotshot over here."

"Seriously?" I quirked a brow at Aaron. "You're an ass."

"Photo time," Mom called, ushering me and Lily over to a huge tree. "Say happy graduation."

Lily smothered a laugh, smiling up at me again.

Fuck, I was going to miss her.

We'd spent time apart over the last four years. Football kept me busy. Especially when the season was in full swing. But this was different. This was the start of our lives together. Our future. And we wouldn't even be in the same state for most of the summer.

"Get in there Jason, Felicity," Mom ordered, and the Fords joined us.

"Proud of you, sweetheart," Jason said as Felicity swiped a tear from her eye.

"Mom," Lily groaned. "You promised."

"I'm allowed to shed a tear or two, baby. We're just so proud of you. Both of you."

My chest tightened. Jason and Felicity weren't only my girlfriend's parents, they were family. And they had never made me feel anything less. Which is why I really needed to talk to Jason before I left.

But every time I went to bring it up, something or someone got in the way.

He squeezed my shoulder, leaning into whisper, "This is it, son. Everything you worked for is finally at your fingertips."

I glanced at Lily and my chest tightened. It had always been football and her. Ever since that seven minutes of heaven in Lindsey Filmer's boat shed, almost five years ago.

But I wasn't ready for the day football took me away from her.

"I love you," she mouthed, eyes twinkling with emotion.

Lily had come a long way in the last four years. She'd grown in confidence, in herself and in our relationship—accepting my endless love for her.

"Love you too," I mouthed back. Not caring one single bit if we had an audience.

She was it for me.

The love of my life.

The woman I intended to spend the rest of my days with.

The woman I wanted to call my wife.

I just needed to make sure she knew that.

Sooner rather than later.

LILY

"What is this?" I asked Mom and Poppy as they wore mischievous grins.

"Your graduation dinner."

Mom wasn't fooling anyone, they were up to something. And I was pretty sure that something was beyond the balloon-lined door of the restaurant they had booked for dinner.

"Dad..."

"Don't look at me," he grumbled. "I had no part in this."

I glanced at Kaiden and he chuckled, looking so handsome in his charcoal slacks and white dress shirt. "I'm as in the dark as you are."

"Hmm." I breezed past them all, entering the restaurant first like the strong, independent woman I was.

There had been a time, back in high school, when I thought I'd never get here. When I couldn't imagine living such a happy, fulfilled life. But here I was.

With a degree to my name, a boyfriend who loved me unconditionally, and a family who supported me no matter what.

I should have been walking on cloud nine. Except any happiness I felt was steeped in uncertainty and doubt knowing that Kaiden was about to embark on the next chapter of his life... without me.

It was only temporary, but I already felt the permanence in my heart. The idea of not being in Kansas with him. Going to sleep with him at night, waking up with him in the morning.

Four years.

Four years with him at Penn State, loving and living, and now it had come to an end. I was so proud of him, of the man he'd become, but I couldn't help but mourn the loss of our college life.

College was safe. We had a routine. We had our favorite coffee shops and bars and restaurants. We had our gorgeous apartment.

Had.

The word clanged through me, realization hitting me again.

Our life at Penn State was over.

Poppy followed me inside, catching up to me and lacing her arm through mine. "I know you didn't want a fuss, but Mom and I thought—"

"Surprise," the word rang out in the restaurant that I now realized was empty except for a small gathering of our friends and family.

"Look at you, babe." Peyton was first to approach me, pulling me into her arms, her big swollen stomach getting in the way.

"But how—"

She flicked her gaze to Poppy who gave a small shrug. "We thought it would be nice to get the whole gang together."

"Get over here, Mr. Football Hotshot," my best friend crooked her finger at Kaiden, and he strolled toward us.

"Looking good, Peyton," he said. "How's she doing?" His eyes dropped to her bump.

"She?"

"It's a girl," I said.

"I'm not so sure. I'm carrying all in the front and my skin is completely dried out. And don't even get me started on all the cheese and salami I want to eat. All the freaking time."

"That's because my boy has good taste." Xander slid his arms around her waist and dropped his chin on her shoulder. "Congratulations."

"Thank you. We didn't expect to see you here," I said.

"Actually, I knew."

I swung my gaze around to Kaiden and gawked at him. "But you said you didn't just now."

"They wanted it to be a surprise." He shrugged.

It shouldn't have mattered. It was a sweet thing to do. But I couldn't shake the feeling that Kaiden had broken one of our cardinal rules by keeping it from me.

You're just feeling extra sensitive, Lily. Snap out of it.

"Thatcher, get the fuck over here," Bryan and Gav lifted their beers as they stood back, letting my family steal our attention first.

Everyone was here. Peyton and Xander. Ashleigh and Ezra. Aaron and Poppy. Sofia and Cole. Bryan,

Gav and their girlfriends, Carrie-Anne and Penelope.

My best friends. The people I loved most in the entire world, all here to celebrate with us.

With me.

"Congratulations, sweetheart." Mom managed to wiggle in between me and Poppy, wrapping her slender arms around me. "We are so proud of you, Lil."

"Thank you, Mom."

She leaned in and brushed the flyaway hairs from my face, whispering, "This is the first day of the rest of your life, baby. And I can't wait to watch you shine."

Emotion caught in my throat, and I swallowed, trying to give myself a minute as she went off to find Dad. But then someone was pressing a champagne flute into my hand and Dad was clinking his glass, ready to make a speech.

Kaiden slipped his arm around my waist and pulled me close. I peeked up at him and he smiled. "I love you, Lily Ford."

"I love you too."

I did, with all my heart.

But the next few weeks were going to be impossibly hard, I already felt the claws of anxiety tightening around my chest.

"Lily, I—"

Laughter filled the air as my father no doubt said something witty. I couldn't hear his words over the blood roaring between my ears though.

I was freaking out.

This was it. The start of the rest of our lives. And I'd never been more terrified.

Kaiden was drafted to the Kansas Wild. He'd done it—his dreams had come true. Come the fall, millions of Americans would watch him all over the country on game day.

I'd always known he was special. That his skill and determination would see him go all the way. He was ready.

But was I?

Being the girlfriend of an NFL star was... Well, it was impossible to imagine. I'd worked on myself a lot during college. Therapy, pushing my boundaries, stepping out of my comfort zone. But I was still the same girl I'd always been. Shy and deeply uncomfortable in the spotlight.

I wasn't ready.

I'd known it the day of the draft, when I'd watched Kaiden announced as a first-round pick for the Kansas Wild. And I knew it now.

We spent so much time focusing on the future yet, now it was here, and all I could think was I hadn't had enough time. With Kaiden. At college. Finding myself. Learning how to be independent.

"And to Kaiden." Dad's voice grounded me. "You did it, son. You made your dreams come true. Now go out there and show the Wild that you've got what it takes to wear their jersey proudly. We're all rooting for you, son. And I know that you're going to do great things up in Kansas."

"Thanks, Jase." Kaiden lifted his drink in the air, the two most important men in my life sharing a moment.

I waited for my father to add something about us, about our relationship, but the words never came. Because Kaiden was on the cusp of being a star.

And maybe that mattered more in this moment.

CHAPTER TWO

POPPY

"WHAT ARE you doing all the way over here?" I asked my sister as she sat on the edge of the celebrations, nursing her drink.

"Just taking a breather."

"Lily, what's wrong?" I slid into the booth opposite her and pinned her with a knowing look.

I knew my sister. I knew all her little tells, and right now, she was all up in her thoughts.

"I can't believe it's here."

"What... Oh, Lily." I reached over and took her hand in mine. "This is a good thing, Lil. You did it. You survived college. You got your degree. You and Kaiden are stronger than ever"—she winced at that and I frowned—"You and Kaiden are stronger than ever, right?"

"Yes. I mean, I think so." She blanched. "Oh God, Poppy. Listen to me. My boyfriend, the love of my life, is heading to the NFL. Instead of celebrating and counting down the days until he gets to live out his childhood dream, all I can think is how it's going to affect me and our relationship."

"Lily, you have nothing to worry about. You know that, right? Kaiden loves you. He loves you so damn much."

"I know that but is it enough? It's the NFL, Poppy." And all that came with it. The fans, traveling away for games, the parties, the glitz and glamour. "I think we both know I don't fit into that world."

"No," I said. "We are not doing this. You, Lily May Ford, are beautiful inside and out, and Kaiden is lucky that he gets to call you his. Don't ever forget that."

"Thanks." She managed a small, uncertain smile.

My sister had come so far from the girl she once was, but I knew she still found it hard sometimes. But her and Kaiden were solid. They would adjust to the changes ahead of them like they always had.

Still, part of me was relieved Aaron had no plans to enter the draft. He loved playing football for the West Chester Golden Rams but our future didn't include pro football. We wanted to take a year out after graduation, travel, see the world, then we wanted to return to Rixon and settle down.

I couldn't wait. A life with my best friend.

As if he heard my thoughts, Aaron found me across the room and smiled, sending my heart into flutters. He came over, pausing at the booth. "What are you two doing all the way over here?"

"Just talking," I said.

"Actually, I'm going to the restroom." Lily slipped out, leaving us alone.

"She okay?"

"I think she's freaking out."

"Understandable." He sat down beside me and slid his arm around my waist, dropping a kiss on my head. "You're worried?"

"I just don't want this to be the thing that undoes all her progress. Kaiden loves her, Aaron. He loves her so damn much."

"I'm sure they'll figure it out. Kaiden is grounded, he won't let the fame and fortune go to his head."

"Honestly"—my eyes flicked over to Lily's receding form—"it's not Kaiden I'm worried about."

Change was hard for everyone, but I knew for Lily it could be so much more. The uncertainty, the unknown. College had become her safety net, her sanctuary, and to have that suddenly taken away...

"Want me to talk to him?" Aaron asked, his expression softening.

"No, I don't think we should meddle. Not yet."

"What?" he asked as I continued staring up at him.

"Does it scare you, the future?"

"Babe, I can't wait for the future." He nuzzled my neck, sucking on the soft skin there as I slid my arms around his.

"Aaron," I murmured.

He pulled away, mischief and lust shining in his eyes. "God, I wish we were alone right about now."

"Behave."

"With you?" He grinned. "Never."

"I love you, Aaron."

"Say it…" His smile got even wider.

"No, I'm not saying it. We're not kids anymore."

"Go on, Poppystar." He leaned in, brushing his mouth over mine. "Say it. You know you want to."

"Fine. Fine. I love you, Aaron the Greatest."

"Damn right, you do." He kissed the tip of my nose. "I love you too, babe. So fucking much."

LILY

I watched them, my sister and Aaron, and couldn't help the smile that tugged at my lips.

I hadn't returned to them after using the restroom. Instead, I lingered in the shadows watching as my friends and family celebrated.

I didn't feel much like celebrating, and I hated it. Hated that I was allowing old insecurities to raise their ugly heads.

"Are you ever going to come and join the party?"

I startled at the sound of my father's voice.

"Hi, Dad," I said.

"Hi, sweetheart." He cast a wary gaze over me. "Wanna talk to your old man for a little bit?"

I really didn't but I knew he wouldn't let me walk away, not now.

He ushered me toward a booth right in the back and waited for me to sit down. "You're not enjoying the party?"

"No, I am. It's just..." I glanced over to where Kaiden was still talking with his friends.

"Talk to me, sweetheart. What's going on in that head of yours?"

"How did you and Mom get through it?"

"Through me playing for the Eagles?" I nodded and he went on. "It wasn't always easy. Pro football is... intense. But I loved your mom, and she loved me, the rest we figured out as we went."

"I'm scared, Dad," I admitted, the words balling in my throat and making it hard to breathe.

"Sweetheart, listen to me, and listen good." He took my hand in his. "Do you think I'd ever let Kaiden hurt you?"

"Dad, come on." I rolled my eyes. "It doesn't work like that."

"Kaiden is a good man, Lily. One of the best. I trust him with your heart, sweetheart. You should too."

Tears threatened to fall. Gosh, I was a mess. But the last few weeks had been such a whirlwind. Finals and packing up our apartment. Now graduation was done. Over.

"You don't have to follow him to Kansas, you know. You can stay—"

"No," I said firmly.

Living apart, doing the long-distance thing was not an option. But I was scared. All caught up in the fear of being in a new town with no friends or colleagues to lean on. Knowing that Kaiden had a team waiting for him. A team who would make him feel welcome and a part of something while I had to start all over again.

"Life is about compromise, sweetheart. You have to work out what sacrifices you're prepared to make for the person you love. It's Kaiden's time to shine right now, but that doesn't mean you have to be eclipsed by his light.

"He's going to need you to, Lil. When practice is hard, when he's trying to prove himself and earn his spot. There's going to be highs and lows and it's going to suck sometimes. He'll need you there to ground him, to remind him that he can do it."

"Did Mom do that for you?"

"Sweetheart, your mom held me together so many times that I honestly don't think I would have made it without her. I thought I had it all figured out in high school, Lily. I thought love was for fools, that it was nothing more than a distraction. But I was wrong. So, so wrong."

Dad looked across the bar to where Mom was talking and laughing with Kaiden's mom.

"Love isn't a weakness, sweetheart. It's something to fight for. Something to live for. And I know you and Kaiden will figure this out. Besides, if he breaks your heart, he knows the deal." A smirk played on his lips.

"Dad!"

"You might be twenty-two, Lily, but you'll always be my little girl and I will always want to protect you."

"I love you, Dad."

"I love you too, sweetheart. Now let's go enjoy your party."

"Okay." I shoved down all the discomfort and

worry and followed him out of the booth and toward our friends and family.

Kaiden spotted me and mouthed, "Everything okay?"

I nodded, mustering the best smile I could.

If I kept lying to him—to everyone—then maybe, eventually the words would come true.

"I can't believe we're all together in the same place," Poppy said, a goofy smile plastered on her face as she laid her head on Aaron's shoulder. "We don't do it enough."

"It's life, Pops," Ashleigh said.

"It sucks. I miss you guys." She pouted at our cousin.

"We have Avery's wedding to look forward to. We'll all be back in town for that."

Kaiden hugged me a little tighter and I knew what he was thinking—that he might not make it. Not with it being right in the middle of football camp. But I was trying not to think about that.

After my little pep talk from Poppy and then my dad, I'd forced myself to put on a smile and enjoy the party.

It was late now though, and the bar staff had started cleaning up around us. None of us were in a hurry to leave though.

Even if I was clinging onto the easy familiarity of being with my friends and family.

"Well, I don't know about the rest of you, but me and Pen will be in Rixon all summer, as usual." Gav chuckled.

"We'll only be home for about three weeks," Cole said, dropping a kiss on Sofia's head. "We want to head North and check out the Lakes."

"Didn't you do enough traveling already?" Aaron grumbled.

"Jealous, Bennet?"

"Of being cooped up in Vera with my sister? Yeah, no."

Everyone laughed.

"How is Vera by the way?" Gav asked Cole and Sofia about their camper van. The one they'd traveled in for almost a year after high school. Now they bounced between Rixon and travelling. When they were home, Cole taught guitar lessons still and did some gigs around the local area while Sofia taught a few classes at the local community center and sold her art online.

"She's good. A little tired around the edges but I think she's got one or two adventures left in her yet."

"You know, Mom and Dad are chomping at the bit for you to put down some roots," Aaron said.

"Maybe, one day." Sofia shrugged. "I like the freedom. The spontaneity."

Something told me it wasn't only that. It was that she didn't like standing still. Maybe more than others, I understood a little bit of what she had gone through.

I hadn't battled a life-threatening illness, but I fought battles against my own mind all the time.

"We're not getting any younger, Sis," he added.

"We have time," Cole said.

Time.

Something I didn't have.

Not when Kaiden left in less than a week.

Sadness washed over me.

God, I didn't want to feel like this. Not when we'd had such an amazing four years.

"Ouch." Peyton rubbed a hand across her swollen stomach.

"Babe?" Xander questioned, concerned.

"He's playing football inside me."

The guys all grimaced while the girls stared at her in awe.

"Here." She grabbed my hand and laid it there. "Can you feel it?"

Sure enough, I felt the faint thud of a foot or a hand. "That is... wow." I smiled.

A baby.

My best friend was having a baby. It still hadn't sunk in. But sitting here with my hand on her stomach, their baby trying to kick his way out, I couldn't deny the truth.

We were getting older. Growing up and moving on to the next stages of our lives.

When all I really wanted was for time to standstill.

CHAPTER THREE

ASHLEIGH

I LAID AWAKE, watching Ezra sleep.

Uncle Jason had checked us all into the hotel down the road from the restaurant for the night.

It was nice of Poppy and Felicity to try and surprise Lily like that, but she didn't look so happy about it. Even before we left, when we'd sat crammed into a booth, reminiscing about days gone by, she'd barely managed a smile.

I wasn't surprised though. Lily was worried about what the future held, about her place in Kaiden's new life.

Part of me got it. Ezra's football career had only gone from strength to strength at Penn State, and success at next year's draft was a good possibility. But Lily wasn't like me.

Even after the accident, even when I had to learn to live with the fact that I had lost almost a year of my life, I soon realized that I was one of the lucky ones.

Life was too short not to embrace it with both hands and enjoy every moment. And with Ezra by my side and my family and friends around me, I had so much to live for.

I pressed in closer to Ezra, trailing my hand down his stomach, loving the way his muscles contracted under my touch.

His hand shot out, grabbing my wrist as I reached the waistband of his boxer briefs. "Don't start something we don't have time to finish," he grumbled, voice heavy with sleep as he slowly cracked an eye open. "Best sight ever."

"You say that every morning."

"Because it's true." He leaned up to kiss me.

"And who said we don't have time? We have time."

"I thought we were meeting everyone for breakfast?"

"We are... in an hour."

"An hour, you say. A lot can happen in an hour." Ezra pounced, rolling me underneath him and caging me in with his big, muscular body.

He'd changed a lot in three years. Bulked out and packed on more muscle. I wasn't complaining. I loved the feel of his weight on me, I loved how safe and delicate he made me feel.

"Good morning." I smiled up at him.

"Good morning." He rocked forward, letting me feel just how happy he was, and a moan slipped off my lips.

"Mmm, you like that, buttercup?"

"You know I do." Wrapping my arms around Ezra's neck, I pulled him down on top of me and kissed him. Soft and teasing, my tongue licked the seam of his mouth, demanding entrance.

He was all too happy to oblige, sliding his tongue against mine, while his hands slipped under the Penn State t-shirt covering my body.

"Fucking love your body, Leigh," he murmured, palming my breast and massaging it. Right then left. Making me whimper and moan.

Shoving the t-shirt up my body, Ezra lowered his head and captured a nipple between his teeth, tugging gently, making me bow off the bed.

"Ah," I cried, digging my fingers into his shoulder.

"Feel good?"

"Mm-hmm."

"Take out my dick. Use me to get yourself off before I fuck you."

"Jesus, E," I breathed.

"Too early for dirty talk?" He smirked and I smothered a chuckle.

God, I loved this man. We'd had a hard and long road in high school, a journey paved with pain and heartache. But we were stronger than ever, and Ezra had spent the last three years making sure I filled the void of a year's worth of lost memories with new ones.

Slipping a hand between us, I pushed his boxers down his hips and freed his length. It was so hard and heavy in my hand, I couldn't resist tugging him a couple of times, loving the low, throaty groan that rumbled in his chest.

"Shit, babe. That's... fuck."

A smile tugged at my mouth as we kissed through the needy breaths and little whimpers as I nudged the crown up against my clit. "God," I panted. "I want you."

"Just a little more. Tease yourself. Get yourself nice and wet for me."

I was lust drunk on Ezra's words, dragging the tip down my center and back up, practically riding the thick length of him. "E," I cried. "I need more. I need..."

"Just a little more. I want to feel you coming right as I fuck into you."

It was my undoing, pleasure cresting over me. But Ezra didn't give me a chance to catch my breath. He hooked his hands under my thighs and slammed into me in one hard thrust.

"Fuuuuck," he groaned, stilling for a second. "You good?"

"Move, I need you to move." He felt too good. Stretching me. Filling me up.

"Love you, buttercup."

"I love you too, so much. Now hurry up and show me. We have to be at breakfast in thirty-five minutes."

"I better make it quick then. Ready?" Challenge sparked in his eyes, and I grinned up at him.

"Always."

KAIDEN

"Morning," Ezra said as he and Ashleigh entered the restaurant.

Only me, Bryan, and Gav had made it down so far. I'd left Lily sleeping peacefully. We'd had a late night, so I hadn't wanted to wake her. But the guys wanted to spend some more time together before they had to head off.

"All good?" Gav asked him.

"Yeah, where is everyone?"

"You know what they're like. They say nine thirty when they actually mean ten." I shrugged.

"You're telling me I could have taken my time—"

"Ezra Bennet, I know you didn't just say that," Ashleigh said from across the room. "Anyone want more juice?"

"Not for me," Bryan said.

"I think we're good," I added, turning to Ezra. "Thanks for coming last night. It meant a lot."

"Any time, you know that." He sat down opposite me, pulling out a chair for Ashleigh.

"Where's Lily and the girls?"

"They'll be down soon."

"Everything good?" she asked me, and I saw the unspoken question in her eyes.

Were things between me and Lily okay?

"We're good."

At least, I hoped we were.

Lily had been quiet last night but when we'd finally gotten back to our room, she'd pressed a kiss to my lips, curled up in my arms and fallen asleep within minutes.

"You think you're ready? Rookie training camp." Ezra grinned.

"I'm ready."

"That's what we like to hear, Thatch," Bryan said. "You down there and show them what you're made of."

"That's the plan."

There were days when I still couldn't believe it. The Kansas Wild. The NFL.

I'd dreamed of nothing since the first day I'd picked up a football and hiked it to my father.

A pang of disappointment went through me, the way it did whenever his name came up. But that was one relationship I had no intention of ever fixing.

Lewis Thatcher was dead to me.

"The NFL, man." Gav whistled between his teeth. "It doesn't get much better than that. Always knew you'd go all the way."

"Thanks."

"It's got to suck leaving Lily behind though," he went on.

"It isn't like they're never going to see each other," Bryan added. "She's moving to Kansas after the summer, right?"

"That's the plan."

Ezra watched me, and I didn't like the intensity in his gaze. The awareness. As if he knew exactly what I was thinking—what Lily was thinking.

"What—"

Voices filled the room and the girls appeared, Lily's parents, Aaron, and Cole in tow.

"Mmm, what smells good?"

"Everything," Gav said. "Everything smells good. Morning, babe." He dragged Pen onto his lap and buried his hand in the back of her hair, kissing her deeply.

"Put the girl down, McKay." Jase grumbled. "It's too early to deal with horny kids."

"They're hardly kids, Jase." Felicity flashed him an amused smile.

"They'll always be kids to me. And I'd appreciate eating my breakfast without watching McKay paw over his girlfriend."

"Sorry, Mr. Ford," Pen chuckled, burying her face in Gav's neck.

Poppy shifted her chair closer to Aaron and he pinned his youngest daughter with a stern look. "Don't you get any ideas Poppy June Ford."

"Dad!"

Our table burst into laughter. Even though his daughters were grown, he was still old school. Which is why I really needed to talk to him. But it seemed whenever I tried, something or someone would get in the way.

Time was running out though. I left for training camp in less than a week.

I was hoping to corner him when we got back to their house later today. The Fords had kindly offered to let me stay with them. It wasn't that I didn't want to stay with Mom, but she lived with Terry now. I was happy for them, I was, but his home would never be my home.

Besides, I didn't want to waste a single second of the little time I have left here without Lily by my side.

"Okay, everyone grab a drink and something to eat. Then I want to say a few words."

"You couldn't do that first, Dad?" Poppy asked.

"I need to eat. Your mom kept me up half the night." He smirked.

"Dad!" Lily gasped.

"With my snoring, sweetheart. Tell them, Jase." Felicity nudged her husband. "Tell them you mean my snoring."

"Whatever you say, babe." He winked at her, heading toward the hot food buffet.

"Your father didn't mean... you know."

I fought a grin as the blush on her cheeks said otherwise.

"Good for you, Mrs. F." Bryan piped up. "Gives me hope for when me and Carrie-Anne are in our late fifties.

"Late-forties," she corrected him.

"My bad, Mrs. F."

"For goodness' sake, Bryan. Call me Felicity, you're making me feel old before my time." She followed Jase, leaving Bryan and Gav staring after her.

"Your mom is a total MILF, Lily."

"Bryan!" Carrie-Anne glowered at him. "That is wholly inappropriate."

"Relax, babe. I'm just joking. It's a joke."

"Not a joke." He mouthed at me over her shoulder.

"I saw that." She snapped.

"Saw what? I was stretching my jaw."

"It's a good thing I love you."

She got up and headed for the buffet counter.

"Not hungry?" I asked Lily who had made no attempt to move.

"Not really."

"You need to eat," I said, leaning in to brush a kiss over her mouth. "Even if you only have something small."

"I'll have some pancakes."

"Atta girl. Come on." I stood, offering her my hand. "Excited to get home to Rixon?"

"I still can't believe it's over."

"End of an era," I said, with a heaviness in my chest.

"It really is. The best four years of my life." Lily gazed up at me with big uncertain eyes.

"But we have so much more to look forward to, Lily. I promise, it's going to be amazing."

I just need you with me on this.

I brushed my knuckles down her cheek, wishing she knew. Wishing that, after all this, it was enough.

But I'd prove her wrong.

I'd show her that it wasn't a choice between football or her. While football was my passion, Lily was my heart.

My home.

And I wanted forever with her.

CHAPTER FOUR

LILY

"HOME, SWEET HOME," Dad said as we filed into the house.

"It feels weird."

"The place hasn't been the same without you and Poppy here, sweetheart. And I know it's only temporary, but me and your mom are excited to have you back for the summer."

"Me too, Dad."

A childhood's worth of memories hit me. Me and Poppy running through the living room, pretending we were unicorns. Forcing Mom and Dad to sit while we performed a dance show—Poppy always the star while I wilted into the shadows. Standing for prom photos in front of the fireplace with Kaiden.

There was so much love and laughter woven into these walls, the very fiber of the house. Even in my darkest moments, as I got older, being here never felt like anything but my sanctuary.

"Thanks for letting me stay," Kaiden said, coming up behind me with our bags.

"It's no problem, son. We have the guest room all set up—"

"Dad!" I puffed out a little sigh.

"He's joking, babe. You are joking, right?"

"Yeah, yeah. I'm joking. Your mom warned me that you're adults now. But you know the deal, Kaiden, this is still my house. And if I catch the two of you—"

"Dad, stop." My cheeks flamed, and a knowing smirk spread across his face.

"Nice to know I've still got it." He winked, heading deeper into the house.

"I'm sorry about him." I glanced back at Kaiden.

"Almost five years, babe." He chuckled. "I think I can handle your old man. I was thinking we could go out tonight. Dinner at La Pomme? Maybe check out Riverside for old times' sake?"

"Or we could stay in," I said. "I'm kind of beat."

"Sure." Something flashed across his face. "Whatever you want."

I was a coward. Avoiding the difficult

conversations. Pretending like everything was okay. But everything felt like it was unraveling, and I was so fixated on the countdown to Kaiden leaving that I couldn't think about anything else.

"Gav mentioned going out with him and Pen too, maybe tomorrow?"

"Yeah, maybe." I hurried down the hall into the kitchen.

"Help a girl out?" Mom asked as she unpacked the groceries they'd stopped for on the way home.

"Sure, Mom," I said.

"Kaiden, be a doll and help Jase take the bags upstairs."

"Sure thing." He studied me for a second but didn't say anything as he slipped out of the kitchen and went in search of my dad.

"Oh, sweetheart, you look so worried. Everything's going to be fine, you know."

"Please, can we not, Mom?"

"Whatever you want, sweetheart. But speaking from experience, the summer camps will be over before you know it and you'll be in Kansas, settling into your new place together. And we have so much to look forward to this summer. Your cousin's wedding. Peyton and Xander's baby. You'll hardly have time to miss him."

I wasn't so sure about that, but I forced a smile on my face.

"You're right, I'm being silly."

Except, I couldn't help but wonder if our relationship would have taken the next logical step if football wasn't in the picture.

Almost five years, and he still hadn't proposed.

I didn't doubt Kaiden loved me. But I'd always imagined that by graduation I'd be wearing his ring. There had been so many moments I'd thought it was coming... and every time, I'd been sorely disappointed.

We talked about the future all the time. The kind of house we'd have one day. How many kids we wanted. Kaiden's dream of having a son to follow in his footsteps.

Once he got drafted, I'd realized it wasn't going to happen. Not yet at least. And I was okay with that. If anyone deserved to live his dreams, it was Kaiden. His work ethic, dedication, and commitment to his team was second to none. But the little voice in the back of my mind had only grown louder over the last few weeks.

Football had eclipsed everything including me. And I hadn't lived in the shadows for so long, it felt disconcerting—suffocating—to be back there.

"Are you excited about the bachelorette party?"

"Oh yeah, drinking and dancing, my two favorite things."

She chuckled. "Come on, Lil. It'll be fun. I for one am excited about a night out in style with the girls. Me, your Aunt Hailee, and Mya have planned a little surprise for the bride-to-be."

"I hope it's not a stripper, because Avery will lose his shit."

"Avery is a big boy, he can handle it." Her lips twitched. "Besides, you think the men won't end up at a strip club after their day on the golf course?"

That made everything inside me go still. "You seriously think they'll go to a strip club?"

"I think it's pretty damn likely." She shrugged. "You know once Kaiden joins the Wild, that kind of stuff is par for the course."

Lovely.

Something else for me to worry about. I trusted Kaiden. I trusted my dad and my uncle to keep the guys in line at Avery's bachelor party. But I didn't know or trust his new teammates. And I guess I'd never really considered that Kaiden might enjoy that kind of thing.

"Oh, sweetheart, I didn't mean—"

"It's fine, Mom," I said, my chest tightening. "I'm going to go help Kaiden unpack, okay?"

"Lily, I didn't—"

But I was already gone, hurrying up the stairs to my room.

To my childhood bedroom—my sanctuary—a place where I would hide when the biggest thing I had to worry about was kids not liking me or teasing me, or me hurting myself.

Not whether or not me and my boyfriend—the man I wanted to spend forever with—were going to survive the next few weeks.

SOFIA

"Hey, you." Cole wrapped me into his arm, dropping his chin to my shoulder as I added a few more strokes to my latest canvas.

"I think this is my new favorite," he said.

"You think? I'm not sure."

"I love it."

Slowly, he turned me in his arms, not caring one bit that I had a paintbrush in my hand.

"Cole," I chided. "I'll get paint—"

He kissed me, drowning out my protests with a teasing flick of his tongue.

"You don't play fair," I murmured, dropping the brush somewhere on the floor behind him so that I could loop my arms around his neck and kiss him deeper.

"I can't wait to be back on the road with you."

A smile tugged at my lips as I broke away to look at him. "I'm excited too."

I loved our simple life in Rixon, but I also loved being out on the road in Vera.

It had been months since our last trip, and I was starting to feel restless.

Life was a bit like that since my stem cell transplant in senior year of high school. Like I was trying desperately to outrun the inevitable. Cram as much life and love and laughter into the time I had before everything went to shit again.

Cole didn't let me dwell. He didn't let fear dictate our lives. Instead, he filled every day with the little things. Waking up to breakfast in bed. Telling me he loved me first thing every morning and last thing every night. He'd supported each and every one of my harebrained ideas over the last three years, and there had been a few. He attended every single doctor's appointment with me. He reminded me to take my medications and vitamins.

He was the perfect boyfriend.

And I honestly couldn't imagine my life without him.

Cole had given up his shot at stardom for me, but I knew in my heart of hearts that he didn't regret it for a single moment. He loved teaching. He loved working with my dad. He loved trying new things and meeting new people. And at the end of a busy week, he loved nothing more than showing me just exactly how much he loved our unconventional life together.

We'd considered college. Cole had even applied. But if what I went through in senior year had taught me anything, it was that life was precious and fragile, and it could all be over in an instant.

I wanted to live.

I wanted to see the world. Experience things. See things. I wanted to be present. To know that if the cancer ever came back that I had zero regrets.

Thankfully, Cole was more than willing to help with that.

"Do you have any idea how much I love you?" he asked.

"I can probably take a good guess."

"Not possible. Just when I think I've hit my ceiling of love for you, you break right through it."

"Breaking the glass ceiling, huh?" I chuckled. "You're such a goofball."

"But I'm your goofball." He ran his nose along my jaw, stealing another toe-curling kiss.

"You are. Let me get finished up here, I want to add this one to my store." I motioned to the canvas behind me.

"Want to go out for dinner? My treat?"

"A date?"

"It can be a date if you want it to be. I was thinking the food trucks down at Riverside."

"Sounds good. Shall we invite everyone?"

"Everyone..."

"Lily and Kaiden? Gav and Pen?"

"I don't mind."

"Invite them. We leave soon, it would be nice to hang out some more."

"On it. Say an hour?"

"I might need ninety minutes. You know what I'm like when I get into it."

Ashleigh's mom Hailee said I was a natural. But sometimes it didn't feel very natural. Still, I liked the peace painting brought me though.

It had been Mom's suggestion. Art therapy could be a useful tool for cancer survivors to explore their thoughts and feelings. I hadn't wanted to attend a group, but Hailee offered to work with me one on one. She was kind and patient and she taught me all about brushstrokes and composition.

That was two and half years ago. I hadn't expected to be selling my art now. I didn't make a lot, but it was enough to pay our way and save toward our next trip.

"Let's say two hours," Cole said with a hint of

amusement. His gaze lingered, the way it did whenever he looked at me. As if he couldn't believe I was still here. That he got to spend his life with me.

It was a feeling I would forever treasure. Being the center of his world. Knowing that he was by my side no matter what the future held.

I loved Cole with every fiber of my being and my biggest wish of all was a long and healthy life with him.

CHAPTER FIVE

KAIDEN

"I THOUGHT I might find you out here," Jase said, joining me on their deck. "Couldn't sleep?"

"Something like that."

"I remember it well, son. The summer before I joined the Eagles. I was a mess. All those years dreaming of it, all the years in high school and college fighting to get one step closer, and then suddenly, it's right within reach." He offered me a glass of whiskey and sat down. "You're going to be fine, Kaiden."

"It's not me I'm worried about."

"Ah, Lily..."

"She's pulling away."

"She's just scared," he said. "It's going to be a big adjustment for both of you."

"Have you talked to her?" I asked him.

"She's my daughter, son. I'm the first great love of her life." Amusement twinkled in his eyes, the way it did whenever he reminded me of that little fact. "Of course she's talked to me about it."

"Any sage words of advice."

"You can have it all, Kaiden. Lily *and* football. It doesn't have to be a choice. Will it be easy? I'd be lying to you if I said yes. But you'll get through it."

"I keep thinking that if I'd have done it sooner, we wouldn't be here, she wouldn't be freaking out..."

"So why didn't you?"

Jase didn't clarify what I was talking about, I guess he didn't need to.

"The timing was never right, and I didn't want her to feel suffocated. College was a huge step for Lily, I didn't want to rush her. I've almost asked you so many times for your blessing."

"You know you have it." The way he said it, without hesitation, made the knot in my chest unravel slightly. "Felicity and I love you like a son. And we see the way you love our daughter. So what's the problem?"

"If I ask now, I'm worried she'll think it's a Band-Aid."

"I get that." He regarded me with those icy-blue wise eyes of his.

Jason was the kind of father I'd always wanted. Firm but fair. Understanding and supportive.

He got it.

He knew what it was like to shoulder the burden of greatness. To try and balance your dreams with everything else important to you.

He was one of the best men I knew, and I could only hope to be even a fraction as good as him. On and off the field.

I dropped my head, rubbing the back of my neck, feeling the weight of responsibility press down on me.

"You have my blessing, son." I lifted my head slowly to meet his certain gaze. "You had it four years ago. You had it yesterday, and you'll have it tomorrow. But you're right, Lily doesn't need a ring on her finger to know you love her."

"I'm so fucking scared."

"Honestly, you'd be inhuman if you weren't. Fear is good, Kaiden. Fear reminds us that we care. That we have something to lose. Something to fight for. Now, I'll try to stay out of your business, but you and Lily need to sit down and talk about this before you leave."

"Yeah, you're right." But it was easier said than done because part of me was terrified that it might be too much for her.

That she might fall back into old habits and push me out instead of letting me in.

I loved Lily down to the core of me and worked hard to show her that every single day. But sometimes her demons roared too loudly.

He leaned over, squeezing my shoulder. "You've got this, son."

"Thanks, that means a lot."

He nodded, draining the remainder of his drink. "Now, come on. We should probably get back in there before they come looking."

"Lily is out for the count."

At least she was when I crept out of bed.

"Shit. I'll never get used to knowing my baby girl is sleeping with her boyfriend under my roof." He stood up, extending his hand. "But if it had to be anyone, I'm glad it's you, Kaiden." I took Jason's hand, letting him pull me up. "I don't doubt that one day, you'll formally become a part of our family but as far as I'm concerned that is just a formality. I just wanted you to know that."

"Jase, I—" I swallowed over the ball in my throat.

"Now, now, don't go getting all emotional on me. I have enough of that with Felicity. Apparently, it's something to do with the early menopause. God help me."

"Can I ask you something?"

"Anything."

"Do you think she'll say yes? When I ask her, I mean."

His expression softened. "Son, I think we both know the answer to that question. There is no doubt that she will say yes but the real question is, are you ready to hear it?"

BRYAN

"Is it strange being back here?" I asked Kaiden as we walked down to Riverside.

It was a little goofy but the two of us—Gav and I—had talked him into coming down here for old times' sake.

"I've been back to Rixon, Bry."

"I know but not like this. Not when you're about to embark on something as huge as the NFL. I mean—"

"That's him. That's Kaiden Thatcher," a voice called from behind us, and Kaiden let out a heavy sigh.

"Busted," Gav snorted, wearing a shit-eating grin. Idiot was loving this.

"I told you this was a bad idea." Kaiden toyed with the peak of his ball cap.

"Too late for that now, asshole," I said, whirling

around to greet the huddle of kids, all gawking in Kaiden's direction. "Autographs are ten dollars a pop."

"He doesn't mean that," Kaiden glowered at me before turning his attention to the six starstruck boys. "Hey, guys."

"Oh my God, it's really you. Kaiden Thatcher. First round pick for the Kansas Wild. This is so freaking cool. Hey, can we get like a selfie or something?"

"Sure. If you hand over your cell phones to my trusty assistants, they'll take the photos." He winked at me.

Fucker.

The kids whipped out their cells and thrust them toward Gav and me. "Cameraman, great," Gav mumbled under his breath.

"Okay, everyone get in here." Kaiden wrapped his arms around the six kids and smiled at us.

"Say Wild on three. One, two, three, Wild." Their shrieks of excitement filled the air as Kaiden scribbled his signature on a couple of torn up pieces of paper one of the kids produced from his pocket.

"Shit, we'll never be able to hang out at the arcade now," Gav said.

"Hotshot over here can pull a few strings and get

them to close the place down for us. Private party for three," I suggested.

"Yeah. Not happening. If we draw an unwanted crowd, we'll leave," Kaiden said, waving the kids off.

"This is how it's going to be now, isn't it? You'll come home for the holidays and have to hide out the whole time to avoid the fans."

"You're an ass." Kaiden shook his head gently, but I saw the uncertainty clouding his eyes. His life was about to change in ways we'd only ever dreamed of—back when we were Rixon Raiders, when going pro seemed like a faraway dream.

But I always knew he would make it. Kaiden had it. The skill and grit and determination. He didn't let it go to his head and he'd always kept his feet firmly planted on the ground.

He was special.

And he was going to fucking kill it in the NFL.

Not that I'd ever give him the satisfaction of telling him that.

"I wonder what the girls are doing?"

"Pretty sure they're getting felt up by the masseuse."

"Lily won't get a massage."

"No, well Carrie will. She fucking loves that shit. Drives me mad, thinking about some pretty boy douche with his hands all over her body."

"You seem awfully upset about this, man," Gav said.

"You would be too if Penny came home and told you all about Miguel with the magical fingers. The only person in our relationship with the magic, is me."

"Feeling a tad insecure there, Bry," he teased, and I flipped him off.

"Jesus, when did we grow up?" Gav raked a hand through his hair. "One minute, we're worrying about winning our next game and who's throwing the party, and the next we're—"

"Worrying about Thatch going off to rookie training camp?" I chuckled, but he didn't look impressed. "You know, for a guy living his actual dream, you don't look very happy."

"It's complicated."

"Nah, it's not complicated. You've got this. And Lily will deal because she loves you."

"Yeah." He grimaced.

"You're really that worried?"

"I don't want to be the reason she slips back into old habits."

"Not going to happen. The girls won't let her. Her parents won't either. She's got this." I clapped him on the back. "You've got this. Now let's go in there"—I flicked my head toward the arcade—"and show some high schoolers how it's done."

"Yeah, okay." Kaiden managed to smile. "Thanks for this, guys. I really needed to get out of my head."

"Don't worry, Thatchman, we got you."

"Holy shit, those kids were brutal." I sagged against the side of the new VR game, wiping my brow.

"They beat us fair and square," Kaiden said.

"That blond kid was unreal. His aim was fucking perfect."

"It's official," Gav grumbled. "We're old."

"Yeah, well, something tells me they won't be going home to sexy-as-fuck women who know how to—"

"Dude!" He clapped his hand over my mouth. "There are kids still present."

I shrugged. "Good! Let them hear and maybe then they'll realize that we're the real winners here."

"You need to get out more," Kaiden said, eyeing me with a mix of amusement and mild disgust.

"Relax, it wasn't like I said anything too graphic."

"They were us once," he added. "Thinking they're invincible."

"If only they knew," I said.

"Yeah."

"Come on." Kaiden headed for the exit. "I could eat a horse."

"Better stick to salad. Those coaches are going to push you to your limit at rookie camp."

"Nah," I said. "Eat it while you can, man. I say go the whole hog and get one of everything."

"You're a little bit wrong, Bry, you know that, right?"

"It's thinking about the future. It's got me acting all crazy. Carrie-Anne mentioned getting our own place the other day. Her parents let it slip; they've been saving up a down payment on a house for her. A fucking mortgage... talk about adulting."

"Shit, man. That's great." Gav grinned, but it quickly melted away. "It is great, right?"

"Yeah. I mean, I start at the high school in a month and Carrie-Anne has a bunch of interviews lined up. But buying a house is... a big commitment."

"You're scared."

"Fuck yeah, I'm scared. We only lived together the last year."

"But you love her?" Gav asked.

"Of course I fucking love her. I'm going to marry her one day."

Caz was it for me.

"So what's the problem?"

"Everything's changing," I said as we spilled out on the promenade.

"Yeah, it is," Kaiden echoed.

"Not us though. Not this. No matter where we end up, we'll always be friends."

"Bry's right," Gav said. "Doesn't matter how big of a star you become, Thatch, we'll never let you forget where you came from."

I slung my arm around their shoulders and grinned. "One hundred percent."

CHAPTER SIX

PEYTON

"WHAT DOES IT FEEL LIKE?" Lily asked me as I sprawled out on the couch, resting my hands on my growing bump.

"Some days, it's like a bad case of gas, then others, it's like the gentle tickle of wings. Then some days, if she's angry, she kicks the crap out of me."

"It's amazing. A tiny little human growing inside of you. Already the size of a cabbage according to your book." Lily closed the page and dropped it on the coffee table.

"Is Xander still nervous?"

"He's excited but I think he's worried about what kind of father he'll be."

"He'll be great."

"I keep telling him that, but childhood was hard for him. He lost his mom, then his dad. It was a tough time." I swallowed over the lump in my throat. "I didn't tell anyone this but when I first found out, I was so scared he wouldn't want it."

"The baby?"

"The baby. Me. A family together." I shrugged, shoving down the lingering uncertainty. Xander had been shocked at first. We both were.

I was on birth control. Starting a family wasn't something we'd really talked about let alone planned. But life had other plans.

"Xander loves you."

"Oh, I know. But sometimes love isn't enough."

The blood drained from Lily's face, and I rushed out, "That's not what I mean, and this has nothing to do with you or Kaiden, Lil. It isn't the same. I swear, I didn't—"

"It's fine. I'm fine." She smiled but it didn't reach her eyes. "I didn't come see you to wallow, I came to talk about all things pregnancy and babies. Have you decided on names?"

"Not yet. Although I'm thinking Calista for a girl and Kingsley for a boy."

"And what does Xander think of King—"

"Xander thinks his son will be called Kingsley over his dead body."

"Hey," I protested. "What's wrong with Kingsley? I think it sounds regal."

He came over and leaned down to press a kiss to my head and then moved down to press one to my swollen stomach. "Daddy's home," he whispered.

"*Daddy's home*," Lily mouthed at me with a hint of amusement.

"I've told him not to say it like that," I said.

"Like what?" Xander looked up, glancing between the two of us.

"It just sounds so... dirty." Lily flushed.

"You do know that's what I'm going to be right. This kid's daddy?"

"I'm well aware of that fact, babe. But you make it sound sexual."

"Jesus." He ran a hand down his face, stalking off toward our kitchen.

"Love you," I called after him, unable to hold in my laughter.

"Kingsley is off the list," he yelled back, and I let out a little huff.

"I liked that one."

"What does Xander like?"

"Clarke, after his dad. Or Galen."

"Galen is cute."

"Yeah, maybe. For a girl he likes Kadie or River."

"River?"

"Yeah." My heart stuttered.

"Peyton, that's—"

"I know," I whispered, painful memories pushing their way to the surface.

When Xander had first suggested it, I thought he was joking. But he'd looked me in the eye and said, "Our lives changed that night. I saved you but you saved me too, and now we've made a person, Peyton. A baby."

Xander wasn't Mr. Romance. He didn't constantly shower me with gifts or romantic messages or grand gestures. So when he did tell me something from the heart, I knew that he meant it. I knew that he'd considered his words, his timing, the delivery.

"I think he's right. If you have a girl, you should call her River. It's perfect." Lily gave me a soft, understanding smile.

"River." I rolled the name around my tongue, a slow smile spreading over my lips. "Yeah, I think I can see it."

"Oh my God, Peyton. A baby." She leaned over and grabbed my hand. "I can't wait to meet him or her. They're one lucky person being born into our family, you know."

We weren't related. Not by blood or by marriage. But I knew exactly what Lily meant.

The Fords and the Chases and the Bennets were a family, and almost five years ago, when the Fords had welcomed me permanently into their home, they'd given me the one thing I'd never had.

Family.

I would be forever grateful for that, and to think my little cabbage would get to be a part of that was everything.

"What's the matter?" Lily asked, noticing the silent tears rolling down my cheeks.

"Nothing, I'm just happy. Hormonal and happy."

"You deserve this, Peyton. You deserve all the happiness."

"So do you, you know." I gave her a warm smile. "I know you're scared about Kaiden going off to camp. But your relationship, the love you share, that will never be replaced, babe."

"I really didn't come here to talk about me and Kaiden."

"I know but I need you to hear what I'm saying. He loves you, Lily. More than anything."

"I know."

She did, I saw it glistening in her eyes.

"But you said it yourself earlier. Sometimes love isn't enough."

"No, babe. No way. I refuse to believe you and Kaiden are anything but endgame."

Her big blue eyes were so sad it broke something inside me.

"I really hope you're right."

I didn't doubt Kaiden. Not a single bit. He loved Lily something fierce, but I knew all too well what she could be like when her negative thoughts got the better of her.

"I am," I said with a little smirk. "Just you wait and see."

XANDER

A father.

I was going to be a father.

I still couldn't quite wrap my head around it. The nursery was decorated. Peyton had watched me build the crib and changing station. And we'd picked out the stroller just the other day. But it still didn't feel real.

I'd watched my brother and Hailee have babies. Jason and Felicity too. But I'd never imagined that one day it would be me.

Fuck.

"You okay over there, *Daddy*?" Peyton wiggled her foot in my lap, and I glanced over at her.

The smirk painted on her mouth was enough to send all the right signals to my dick.

"Say that again," I drawled.

"I said, 'are you okay over there, *Daddy*?'" Heat blazed in her eyes as she ran her foot along my junk, making sure to add enough pressure that I felt it that time.

"Don't start something you can't finish," I warned.

"Who says I can't finish it?" Her brow lifted, that gorgeous mouth of hers twitching.

"Last time I tried to get lucky, you called me a selfish bastard, threw the pillow at my head, and cried for an hour straight."

"I was having a bad day." Peyton stuck her tongue out at me.

"A bad day, is that what we're calling it?" I teased.

Pregnancy hormones had turned my girlfriend into a raging psycho. Some days, she was on top of the world, glowing inside and out. Other days, I couldn't so much as breathe without annoying her.

"So you don't want to..." She dragged her foot across my dick again, making the damn thing jolt with pleasure.

"Peyton," I warned.

"Yes, *Daddy*." Her eyes were slight with mischief and lust and love. So much fucking love.

It was hard to believe she was mine. That she loved me. All my jagged broken pieces.

"God, I can't wait to see you with him," I said, running my hand over the curve of her foot, massaging her.

She practically purred, stretching out on the sofa like a damn house cat as I massaged her foot. "That feels so good. Don't stop."

"Mmm, talk dirty to me." Laughter rumbled in my chest.

"You really think it's a boy?"

"I hope so."

I'd imagined a son since she broke the news to me. I was terrified, yes. But determined to be a better father than I had been a young man.

"And if it's a girl..."

"Then God help me, and God help any guy who ever tries to come within ten feet of her."

"Hmm, why is that such a turn on?"

"Oh yeah, you like that? The protective dad routine?"

"I don't hate it." Peyton batted her lashes at me.

She made pregnancy look so effortless. Sure, she was hormonal and grumpy sometimes, but she made it work.

Silence settled between us as I stroked her foot

back and forth. Until a soft sigh slipped from her lips, and I asked, "What's wrong?"

"Are you scared?"

"Scared?"

She nodded. "That we're not ready? That I'm too young? That it isn't the right time?"

"I'd be lying if I said I wasn't scared. It's a baby. It doesn't get much bigger than that. But we're ready."

It had taken a while for everyone to get used to the idea. But ultimately, it wasn't their decision what we did with our lives. Besides, Hailee was only twenty-two when she and Cameron had Avery and they'd gotten through it.

"How do you know?"

"Because we love each other. Because one day, you'll be Mrs. Peyton Chase. Because we both know how precious and fragile life is."

Her expression softened. "I already love her or him so much it terrifies me."

"Scared is good," I said. "Scared means you care."

"This has been a good talk, babe. But are you going to sex me up now? I'm horny."

"Think I already did enough sexing you up." I arched a brow, running a hand over her bump.

"Xander! Unless you want me to think you no longer find me attractive, please stop talking and come kiss me."

"You're extra bossy tonight."

"Horny, babe. I'm extra horny. You should make the most of it before it passes."

"Well, yeah when you put it like that." Lifting Peyton's legs off my lap, I slipped out from under her and lay beside her on our giant sectional.

"Hi." She gazed up at me.

"Hi."

Peyton wiggled closer, sliding one of her legs over mine. I pulled it higher, anchoring it at my waist. "Touch me, Xander. I won't break."

"The bab—"

"Is fine. I'm fine. We're all fine. But I'm going to be one pissed pregnant woman if you don't... Give. Me. What. I. Need... in the next ten seconds."

"So demanding." I slid my hand higher, slipping it under her sleep shorts to grab a handful of her ass.

"That feels nice."

"What about this?" I dipped my fingers into her, plunging them deep.

"Yes... God, yes. Touch my clit too."

I snorted at her breathy command. "I do remember how to get you off, you know."

"So stop talking and do it."

Gently, I wrapped my hand around Peyton's throat, and kissed her hard while my fingers curled inside her.

"Yes... more..." she murmured.

"My greedy girl."

"You, I want you." Peyton pushed her fingers into the back of my hair, kissing me deeper.

I needed to fuck her. To feel her pussy clenched around me. It had been too long.

"You sure?" I asked.

"Xander, I swear to God. If you don't fuck me in the next two seconds..."

"Face the other way." I helped her get into position, wrapping my arm around her chest, and using my hand to lift and hook her leg around me.

Brushing my fingers over her clit again, I kissed up her neck, making sure she was desperate and ready for me.

"Xander, stop teasing me and— Ah," she cried out as I rocked into her.

It was a tight fit in this position, but it felt incredible.

She was incredible.

"Feel good?" I rasped, licking and biting her throat as I found a slow, steady pace that worked for her.

"So, so good." Eyes closed, lips parted with ecstasy, Peyton rocked back against me,

Letting the waves of pleasure carry her away.

CHAPTER SEVEN

LILY

"WHERE ARE WE GOING?" I glanced over at Kaiden, and the corner of his mouth tipped.

"It's a surprise."

"You know how I feel about surprises."

He reached over and grabbed my hand, smoothing his thumb over my skin. "I think you'll like this one."

I suppressed a shiver. Sometimes, when he looked at me like that, I felt it.

Our future.

Our love story.

Kaiden loved me, I didn't doubt that. But in the days since we'd moved back to Rixon, my mind had become the enemy. Whispering to me. Reminding me that he was about to embark on something life changing.

Kaiden was already a star in his own right. You didn't lead your team to the NCAA championship twice, and break the all-time passing yards record, without earning some level of notoriety.

Just yesterday, he and my dad had caused a ruckus in town. Seeing Jason Ford walk the streets of downtown Rixon was one thing but to see him walking beside one of the most successful NCAA players of our recent years was too much for people to deal with.

Kids had swarmed them, asking for autographs and photos while Mom and I stood on the sidelines.

That was destined to be our story—him, the football star, me, his completely average girlfriend.

"How was Peyton?"

"She was okay, big and uncomfortable. But she's almost there. It's strange," I let out a soft sigh. "When she first told me, I couldn't imagine it. We're so young."

"Hailee and Cameron had Avery when they were the same age, didn't they?"

"They did. But that was different. Cameron practically helped raise Xander. Peyton is my best friend. She's still the party girl with a penchant for trouble."

"Except, she isn't that girl anymore," he said.

"No, I guess she isn't."

But she would always be the girl I'd watched live her life unapologetically. Despite everything she went through with her mom, Peyton always lived life to the fullest.

God, I'd envied her back then. Her ability to walk into the room and steal the show. Even now, she made pregnancy look effortless. But that was Peyton. She had the ability to adapt. To take everything in her stride.

"One day, babe," Kaiden said, and I frowned over at him.

"What?"

"One day that'll be us."

My heart spluttered in my chest. Had he really just said that?

"Lily," he added. "What's wrong?"

"You just surprised me, is all."

"We've talked about the future before."

"I know." We had. But only in the way that most college couples made plans for the future.

What-ifs, dreams, and maybes.

"Lily, do we need to talk about this?"

"I don't know, do we?"

"This was always the plan." Kaiden ran his hands

around the wheel, frustration bleeding from his expression. "Football is..."

"Everything to you, I know."

"Lily, come on. You know that's not... Fuck." He pulled over to a rest area and cut the engine. "I know you're scared," he said, twisting around to look me dead in the eye.

"I'm not—"

"It's okay. I'm scared too. I'm scared that I'm not going to fit in. That I won't be good enough."

"You're good enough, Kaiden. You know you are."

"But I'm still scared. I'm moving to a new town, a new team. And I'm doing it all without you by my side. I don't like this either."

"I..." I pressed my lips together, trapping all my insecurities and doubts. He didn't need me to add to the pressure. Reaching over, I laid my hand on his cheek. "You're going to be amazing."

"You think?"

"I know so. You've got it, Kaiden, and I have no doubt you'll go to Kansas and earn your spot on the team. Your dream came true, babe. You did it."

His eyes clouded over a little as he stared at me, the air thick between us.

"I can't do it without you by my side, you know that, right?" His hand slid into my hair, drawing me closer, until I could feel his warm breath on my face. "I need you, Lily. And I know things have been different between us since I was drafted. I know you're scared, but the way I feel about you, the life I want with you, that hasn't changed.

"It will never change."

"Kaiden..."

I didn't want to do this, not now. On the side of some road leading out of Rixon.

"I love you," he went on. "I love you so fucking much. It's a few weeks, Lily, and then it's just you and me, babe."

Except, it wasn't.

It was me, him, and the Kansas Wild.

"Say something," he whispered, touching his head to mine.

"I love you and I'm so, so proud of you."

It didn't feel like enough, not after his words—his promises—but it was all I had.

"Come on, we have a reservation." Kaiden kissed me, soft and lingering, his lips curving into a smile.

God, I loved that smile. It made my heart flutter every time he aimed it in my direction. It lifted my spirits in the days when my mental health got the better of me.

He was my rock. My best friend. My everything.

And in two days, I would lose him to his dream.

I smiled as The Nook came into view, I couldn't help it.

"I'd forgotten how pretty it is out here," I said.

We'd only been out here once before. It was Cole and Sofia's favorite place to go to and when she finally got the all-clear after her stem cell transplant a few years ago, we'd come out here to celebrate with them.

It was a big cabin style restaurant, deep in the woods with a wraparound porch and wide stairs leading to a set of double doors framed with glass. The whole place radiated rustic chic, and from what I could remember, the food was amazing.

Inside, the focal point was the big open fireplace on the back wall, roaring away despite the balmy air. Beyond the windows was a firepit area that was littered with hand-carved benches and swings and a beautiful wooden pergola covered in creeping vines.

It was the perfect romantic hideaway, and I was both surprised and touched that Kaiden had brought me out here.

"I thought you'd like it," he said, cutting the engine and coming around to open my door. "Come on."

Kaiden grabbed my hand and gently tugged me along. Maybe it was my mind playing tricks on me, but he seemed nervous.

Because it's almost goodbye.

I shut off the little voice. I didn't want to ruin the night, I wanted to enjoy a romantic meal with my boyfriend and worry about the rest later.

The only problem was my mind had other ideas.

KAIDEN

"How was everything?" the server asked as she collected up our plates.

"It was lovely, thank you." Lily smiled, looking lighter than she had in days.

I'm glad she felt relaxed because I was a bag of nerves. I'd barely been able to digest the prime rib thanks to the small ring box burning a hole in my pocket.

It was tonight.

After my chat with Jase, I realized I didn't want to wait. I shouldn't have waited so long in the first place. I loved Lily with everything that I was, and I wanted to leave for camp knowing that she was mine.

Today. Tomorrow. And all of the days after.

But fuck, I was nervous.

Put a ball in my hand and a hundred thousand fans in the stands and I was in my element. Put a small ring box in my pocket and I was a bumbling, nauseous idiot.

It's just Lily. She loves you. She. Loves. You.

"Everything okay over there?" she asked when the server left us.

"Fine." I grabbed my beer and drained the remainder of the contents. "Just a little hot."

"It is warm in here. The open fire is beautiful, but they could do with better a/c. How was your food?"

"Good. It was good."

"Kaiden, look, I know I've been—"

"Shall we go outside? Check out the singer?"

Live entertainment was one of the big draws of the place. People came from all over the local towns to watch their musicians sing, serenade, and play.

"But dessert."

"I'll ask them to bring it out to us."

"Oh, okay." She smiled again but this time it didn't quite reach her eyes.

If she suspected I was up to something, this would be the last thing on her mind.

Part of me hated that, hated that she automatically assumed the worst.

I'd never given her cause to doubt me, not once.

But I knew it wasn't that simple. And I knew that me leaving soon weighed heavily on her mind.

I waved over the server and ordered our dessert, requesting that it be brought to us outside. Of course, Lily didn't know that they were already in on the secret.

Fuck.

My heart thudded in my chest as I stood, taking Lily's hand. This woman was going to be my wife one day. The mother of my children. The woman I'd grow old with.

I'd known it when we'd left for college together and I knew it now. And part of me was desperate to get it over with. To slide the princess cut ring onto her finger and erase every doubt she had about us and what the future held.

Football was my passion. It was the thing I excelled at. A childhood dream come true. But Lily... she was my home. My heart. The other half of my soul.

"Kaiden?" she asked, casting me a strange look.

I leaned down and brushed my mouth over her jaw, giving her a lingering kiss. "Come on," I said, leading her out of the cabin.

The singer was a young guy with a deep, raspy voice that held everyone's attention. We slid onto the hand-carved bench, and I wrapped my arm around

Lily. She laid her head on my shoulder, tapping her foot to the moody song about love and loss and longing.

Jesus, where was dessert? The sooner I did this, the sooner I could relax. Celebrate with the future Mrs. Thatcher.

Damn, that sounded good.

I realized now, I shouldn't have waited. I should have put a ring on Lily's finger in freshman year. But we were young, and it was such a feat for Lily to even be at college, I didn't want to pile on the pressure. I wanted her to spread her wings, to experience life. To soak up the college experience. Then somewhere along the way, waiting until after graduation seemed like the right thing to do.

Dessert took longer than I expected, every second painfully slower than the last. Lily was content, nestled into my side, listening to the singer. But I barely heard a word over the blood roaring between my ears.

"Are you sure you're okay?" Lily gazed up at me. "You seem really tense."

"I'm fine." I smiled, trying to force the tension out of my expression. "He's good."

"Yeah." Lily looked back at the singer who was taking a short break. "Oh, I think our dessert is here."

I glanced over to find the server heading toward us.

Shit. This was it.

"Lily," I took her hand in mine. "I just want you to—"

"Sorry." She pulled her vibrating purse onto her lap and dug out her cell phone. "It's Mom." Lily flashed me an apologetic smile as she answered. "Hi, Mom. What... slow down, I can't— No. Oh God, okay, he's... Yeah. We're on our way."

"What's wrong?" I asked, a sinking feeling going through me.

The server arrived with the perfect dessert for my perfect moment.

"Sorry, we have to leave," Lily rushed out, fear etched into her expression.

"But your dessert, the—"

"It's Peyton," she said. "She's gone into labor."

CHAPTER EIGHT

ASHLEIGH

"LILY, THANK GOD." I rushed over to her, wrapping her into my arms.

"How is she? The bab—"

"We don't know much yet. Xander's with her though. Your mom is trying to get some answers. God, Lil, what if—"

"She's fine. They'll both be fine." Lily nodded. "The baby is almost thirty-two weeks, even if she comes now, her odds are good. They'll be fine."

"She must be terrified."

Kaiden came up behind Lily and laid his hands on her shoulders, squeezing softly. "They're in the best place."

"We were at The Nook. We came as soon as Mom called."

"Come on, let's go sit down," I suggested, glancing at Kaiden again.

He looked crestfallen. We were all worried, of course. Peyton and Xander were family and everyone was so excited about the baby.

But it was too soon. There could be complications. All kinds of problems if the baby came now.

A shudder went through me, and Lily squeezed my hand. "Where's Ezra?"

"He and Jase are getting coffee. It's going to be a long night."

There was no chance of any one of us leaving yet, not until we knew Peyton and the baby were okay.

"Mom and Dad are on their way," I said. "Mom had an event at the gallery."

"Hey," Ezra appeared, handing me a cup of coffee. "Any news?"

"Nothing."

"Come on, let's sit." He guided me over to the row of plastic chairs and we sat down. Him on one side and Lily on the other. Kaiden sat down next to her.

"Your dad went to find your mom and see if they can get an update."

"I can't believe this is happening," Lily said. "I only saw her a couple of days ago and she was fine."

"Lily, thank God," Aunt Felicity said as she and Uncle Jase appeared at the end of the hall. Lily got up and went to them, letting them wrap her up in a hug. I laid my head on Ezra's shoulder and he gently squeezed my knee.

"Anything?" I asked, as the three of them came closer.

"Nothing yet. They've promised somebody will update us as soon as possible."

"God, this is horrible," I said.

"It's a waiting game. But they're in the best place," Uncle Jase said. "I'm going to call Asher and let them know what's happening."

"I've already texted Poppy," Lily added.

"I wish I could be in there with her." Aunt Felicity stared down the hall toward the doors marked restricted access.

"She'll be okay, Mom." Lily reached for her mom's hand, tears clinging to their lashes.

None of our parents had been happy when Peyton and Xander announced their relationship. She had been young—still in high school—and Uncle Xander had been the football team's assistant coach. But Peyton wasn't like most other seniors. She'd lived through things no kid should. Been forced to grow up way too quickly.

It had taken time for them to accept it. To welcome Peyton into the fold as Xander's girlfriend and not their daughter's best friend.

But Aunt Felicity had always retained some deep sense of protectiveness over the girl they took in when she had nowhere else to go.

"I hope so, sweetheart," she said quietly. "God, I hope so."

Everyone was sleeping when I sensed someone approaching. We'd been out here hours, waiting for an update.

My eyes fluttered open and I found Xander walking toward us, but his expression was clouded over.

"Xander? What is it?" Dread snaked through me as I bolted off the chair. "Are they—"

"It's a girl. I... I have a daughter."

"Oh my God, she's here?" I threw my arms around him, tears rolling down my cheeks.

"Congratulations. I'm so— Xander?" I pulled away to look at him.

"She's so tiny, Leigh." His voice cracked, the blood drained from his face. "They took her away to be monitored."

"That's good, Xan. They need to make sure she's strong enough. Peyton, is she—"

"She was amazing. But she lost a lot of blood."

"Oh my God, will she be okay?"

"They said she'll be okay. I should probably get back in there. But she wanted me to tell you all that she's okay. They both are."

"Tell her we're all here, waiting to see her."

"I will." He nodded, still looking a little dumbstruck.

"Xander?" I asked when he didn't move.

"I... shit, I don't know what to do. She's so fucking tiny, Leigh Leigh." He began to tremble.

"Hey, it's okay." I hugged him again. "It's okay, Xan. You don't need to do anything other than go back in there and be with your girls, okay?"

Inhaling a shuddering breath, he nodded again. "I can do that."

"Of course you can. And as soon as Peyton is up for visitors, we'll be there."

"I have a daughter, can you fucking believe that?"

"You should go." My smile grew. "She needs her daddy."

His eyes widened a little at that.

"You've got this, okay?"

"Thanks, Leigh Leigh. I was freaking out there for a minute."

"Go," I urged. "I'll tell everyone." I glanced at the row of sleeping people.

"Yeah, okay." Xander nodded and took off back down the hall.

"Was that—"

"A girl, Aunt Felicity." I sucked in a sharp breath, trembling. "They have a baby girl."

"Oh my God, really?" Tears pooled in the corners of her eyes, and I nodded over the lump in my throat.

Everyone began to stir.

"What's going on?" Lily asked.

"She's here. The baby is here." I grinned.

"S-she? It's a girl?"

"It's a girl. We have a baby girl."

Because I didn't doubt this baby was ours. Peyton was our best friend. The family we chose. And now she and Xander had a baby.

A daughter.

"That's great news," Kaiden said, pulling Lily to

his side and dropping a kiss on her head. "Are they doing okay?"

"They've taken baby away to be monitored and Xander said Peyton has lost a lot of blood."

"Well, that doesn't sound too good," Uncle Jase said, running a hand over his jaw. "I'm going to speak to a nurse."

"Come here." Ezra stood and wrapped me in his arms. "You good?"

"Just worried about them. And Xander. I think he was in shock."

"He's got this, Leigh."

"Yeah." I gazed up at him, imagining the day this was us. At the hospital, welcoming our baby into the world.

"What?" he frowned.

"Nothing." A small, secretive smile tugged at my lips.

I wanted that. I wanted it all with Ezra. But for now, I was content with him being the person I turned to. The person who held me when things got too hard.

I'd loved Ezra Bennet since the moment he arrived in Rixon, and I would love him for the rest of my life.

KAIDEN

The next morning, we were finally allowed in to see Peyton.

"Lily," she croaked from the bed.

Lily rushed over, grabbing her best friend's hand and situated herself in the chair Xander vacated.

"Oh my God, Peyton. We've been so worried."

Xander made his way over to me and held out his hand. "Thanks for staying," he said.

"Of course, if you need anything..." I let the offer hang.

"Thanks."

"How is she?" I slid my gaze toward the girls.

"Exhausted. Worried about River."

"You named her?"

"We did." He smiled proudly. "River Cadence Chase."

"Congratulations, man."

"I still can't believe she's here."

I clapped him on the shoulder. "Believe it, Xander. Life is never going to be the same again." A heavy kind of silence settled between us and then I asked, "She's good though, right? The baby?"

"She's in the NICU. She's so fucking tiny and fragile but the doctors said she's strong. Just like her mama."

Xander gazed at Peyton with a look of awe. Her eyes found his and the two of them shared a moment.

"I can't wait to meet her," Lily said, still clutching Peyton's hand.

"You can, soon. You can't go into the room yet, but they have an observation window. Xander will take you later."

"Oh my God." My girl was crying, big fat silent tears rolling down her cheeks, our date night all but forgotten.

Except, I hadn't forgotten. The ring had burned a hole in my pocket the entire ride to the hospital.

I'd waited too long to ask her, and now, my chance had passed us by. But I couldn't regret it, not when I knew how much Lily needed to be here for Peyton and Xander.

I only regretted that we didn't have some news of our own to share with them.

Maybe it was the universe's way of saying it wasn't the right time.

I didn't want to believe that but fuck, if I didn't believe everything happened for a reason. There was no way I could ask her now. Like the good friend she was, Lily would be glued to Peyton's side, one hundred percent ready to do whatever needed to be done to help the new mom and baby.

"Oh God, Avery's wedding," Peyton cried. "We'll

probably have to miss it."

"That doesn't matter," Lily said. "All that matters is that you heal, and River gets stronger. Avery and Miley will understand."

"There's still time." Xander approached them.

"How are you feeling?" he asked Peyton.

"I'm okay. A little tired. But okay. I just wish she was here with us. It doesn't feel right that she's all by herself."

"I'll take you down to her soon."

"We should go, we can come back another time."

"No, no, don't leave, not yet." Peyton squeezed Lily's hand. "Having you here helps distract me. The last sixteen hours have been surreal."

Just then, the door opened, and Jason and Felicity slipped inside. "Room for two more?"

"Of course, guys, come in."

"We just wanted to say bye. Cameron and Hailee just got here so we're going to head home."

"But if you need anything..." Felicity stood behind Lily and smiled at Peyton.

"Thank you."

"You did so good, sweetheart. So, so good. And that daughter of yours is a fighter. She's strong, just like her mommy and daddy."

"I hope so."

"Try and rest, okay? You're going to need it for

the coming weeks. We'll come visit again soon."

"I'll walk you out," Xander said, dropping a kiss on Peyton's head before following Jason out of the room.

Lily got up and hugged her mom and she followed them out.

"You look tired," Lily said to Peyton.

"The doctors said that's common. I'll be okay. It's River I'm worried about."

"Mom's right, babe. If she's anything like you, she's a fighter. Get some rest, we'll come back soon."

"You don't have to go."

"I'm sure Uncle Cameron and Aunt Hailee will want to spend some time with you both. I'll call Xander later and see how you're all doing."

Peyton nodded, her eyes heavy and tired.

Lily came to my side, and I took her hand, sliding my fingers through her own. I couldn't help but glance at her ring finger, a pang of regret going through me.

But I locked it down.

Today wasn't about me—about my hopes and dreams. It was about Peyton and Xander. About the premature baby girl lying in the NICU.

There would be other opportunities.

Other perfect nights.

I just had to figure out a new plan.

CHAPTER NINE

XANDER

I DIDN'T THINK it was possible to love someone more than I loved Peyton.

Until I laid eyes on our daughter.

Fear like I'd never known had practically crippled me when Peyton had called me two days ago to say her water broke.

It was too early.

We were only thirty-two weeks along.

If the baby came now there was a high risk of all kinds of complications.

Turns out that our baby girl was a fighter. And although she only weighed four pounds six ounces, and needed to remain in the NICU for observations, she was perfect.

I still couldn't get my head around it.

I had a daughter.

This tiny little thing that depended on me to raise her.

Jesus. I wasn't prepared for this.

But maybe that was the beauty in becoming a parent—you could never be fully prepared. It was one of those things you had to experience. No amount of research or reading or support could fully prepare you for what was to come.

"Xander?" Peyton murmured and I leaned forward, rubbing my hand over her forehead.

"It's okay, you were sleeping."

"River?"

"She's fine. I just came back from the NICU. She's been fed. Doctors are pleased with her progress."

"She's okay?" Tears clung to her lashes.

"She's okay." I nodded, taking Peyton's hand in mine and bringing it to my lips. "How do you feel?"

"I'll feel better once I see her. I hate this."

"I know. But she needs to get strong. I'll take you down soon, okay? First you need to eat something."

"I'm not—"

"Leaving this room until you eat something."

"Fine."

"Fine."

She glared at me but I didn't back down. Peyton needed to get her strength up too. I needed both my girls to be as fit and healthy as possible.

"You need to eat," my voice softened as I stroked the back of her hand.

"I said I will."

"Good." I leaned over, kissing her brow. "Everyone has been checking in. They're all desperate to meet her."

"I want them to meet her when she's healthy."

"Peyton, the doctors said—"

"I know what they said but she's not here, with us. Until then, I don't want everyone..." She trailed off, the tears breaking free.

"Shh." I squeezed her hand. "It's okay. We can take things slow."

My brother and Hailee had already met River. Lily and Kaiden too. But our family was big and from all the texts and calls I'd been fielding all morning, they were all eager to meet our new arrival.

"I just want to hold her. I'm supposed to be the one holding her."

"You held—"

"It's not the same, and you know it." Frustration bled into Peyton's words. And I hated it. I fucking hated that she felt anything but the goddess she was.

But I also understood.

Peyton thought her body had failed her—had failed River. She blamed herself, and no matter how much I tried to reassure her that wasn't the case, I knew it didn't matter.

"Look at me." I gently gripped her chin, forcing her big blue eyes to mine. "I'm in fucking awe of you, babe."

"Y-you are?" Her lip wobbled and I slid my thumb along the seam.

Even now—sleep-deprived and mentally exhausted—she was beautiful.

"Yes. Now, I know you're scared. I am too. But the doctors said she's strong and that with a little care and attention, she'll come out the other side of this, okay?" Peyton nodded. "So let's get some food into you, get you cleaned up a bit, and then go see our baby girl."

A faint smile ghosted her lips. "Okay. And Xander?"

"Yeah?"

"Thank you."

"No, thank you." I leaned in, touching my head to hers. "You gave me something I never imagined, Peyton. A family."

And I planned on never letting them go.

LILY

"Hey." Kaiden slipped his arms around my waist and nuzzled my neck, sending licks of heat down my spine.

"Mmm, good morning to you too. Good workout?"

"Yeah. I ran circles around Gav." He chuckled. "He sends his love. Pen too."

"You saw Pen?"

"And Millie and Pen's brother, Max. They dropped Gav off."

"Oh."

"You could have come—"

"Running?" I balked. "I don't think so. I've been making Peyton and Xander some meals for when they get home."

"That's nice."

"It's the least I could do. They're going to have their hands full." I dried my hands on the towel and turned in Kaiden's arms. "I can't believe you leave tomorrow."

Dread snaked through me.

"We still have the entire evening. I thought we could try date night again, if you're feeling up to it?"

"I... I think I'd rather stay in."

"Oh, okay." Disappointment glittered in his eyes.

"I know it's your last night," a soft sigh rolled through me, "but with Peyton in the hospital—"

"It's fine, I get it. Maybe we can have a romantic night in." He lowered his mouth to mine, brushing a featherlight kiss over my lips. "Your mom and dad said something about going for dinner at the Bennets'."

"Yeah, maybe."

It was hard to concentrate on anything knowing that my best friend and her baby were in the hospital, and my boyfriend left tomorrow for training camp.

Kaiden watched me, searching my eyes for answers I didn't have.

"Sorry"—I forced a smile—"my head is all over the place."

"I know." He kissed my forehead. "I wish I didn't have to leave tomorrow, but I—"

"It's okay. We both knew this day would come."

I wish I could say it had crept up on us, that we hadn't had all the time in the world to prepare—to talk over our worries and concerns. Well, mainly mine.

But fear was the enemy, and the little voice in my mind encouraged me to pretend everything was fine rather than facing things head on.

"It's only one summer, Lil. One summer, then we have forever."

Forever, God. It was all I wanted.

A life with Kaiden. A future. A home.

"Forever." I whispered, too scared to ruin the moment. To give my ugly thoughts power.

We would get through the next few weeks, I would move to Kansas, and everything would be fine.

If I kept saying it enough, maybe it would come true.

"Lily, what's wrong?" Kaiden asked as he joined me on the couch for movie time.

"Look." I held up my phone, tears rolling down my cheeks.

"They got to hold her."

I nodded. "Look at them."

The photo of Peyton and River having skin to skin was one of the cutest, albeit surreal, things I'd ever seen.

"She's so tiny. Look at her little fingers."

"She's all Peyton." Kaiden got comfy and curved his arm around my shoulder, drawing me into his side.

"You think? I can't really tell." Her features were

too delicate yet, her skin paper thin. But he wasn't wrong, she was beautiful just like her mama.

"She's a cutie but don't go getting any ideas." He chuckled but it only made my blood turn to ice. "Lil?"

"Shall I play the movie?"

"Hey." His fingers slid under my jaw, angling my face up. "What's wrong?"

"Do you really have to ask?"

"I know, babe. I know." His expression softened. "But it's only a few weeks."

I wanted to tell him a lot could change in a few weeks, that maybe he'd change. Maybe he would realize that he wanted other things. Different things. But that was the little voice in my head. The one that had been growing louder and louder ever since the moment he'd been drafted.

"Yeah, I know." I kissed him. The perfect distraction to the words I couldn't say.

We snuggled down and Kaiden pressed play on the movie. But I barely caught a thing, too lost in my thoughts.

Kaiden's touch kept me grounded though, his fingers stroking my arm then my hair.

I was at war with myself. On the one hand, I wanted to lose myself in him tonight. To imprint our last night together on my mind so that I could get through the summer. But on the other hand, it hurt too much to think about saying goodbye to him this way.

"Mmm, you taste good." he drawled, dragging me up and onto his lap. His fingers slid into the back of my hair as he deepened the kiss.

"Kaiden." I fisted his t-shirt unsure whether to push him away or pull him closer.

Winding his hand into my hair, he gave me a gentle tug. The air turned thick, making it hard to breathe.

Or maybe it was the way he looked at me. With pure hunger.

"How long until your mom and dad get home, do you think?"

"We can't," I said. "Not down here."

"You want to move this upstairs then?"

"I... okay."

We got up and Kaiden made quick work of turning off the TV and locking up. With every step I took up the stairs, my heart crashed violently against my chest.

This was it.

The moment I'd been dreading.

Our final night together.

God, I was going to cry.

But then I felt him behind me. Kaiden looped his

arm around my waist and pressed in close, stopping me at the top of the stairs. "I love you, Lily May Ford."

"I love you too." I twisted my face to look at him.

His eyes turned cloudy again, a faraway expression washing over him. I'd noticed it a couple of times now. It was strange because Kaiden always seemed so sure of himself. But he almost seemed... nervous.

"You're going to be great," I said, reassuring him.

"What?" Confusion fell over his face.

"Tomorrow," I explained. "You're going to be great."

"Tomorrow, yeah."

"Kaiden?"

"Come on. I want to make the most of our last night together." He took my hand and moved ahead of me.

We'd stayed in my room a lot over the last four years. It was a part of our story, one of the places I'd fallen in love with him.

"You're trembling," Kaiden said as we entered my bedroom.

"I... I'll be fine."

He closed the door and drank me in. It was impossible not to feel beautiful when Kaiden looked at me. It was one of the things I loved most about him, the way he constantly tried to build me up.

"Come here." He crooked his finger at me, and I went willingly.

How could I resist?

The answer was, I couldn't. This man owned my heart.

Every last piece.

He'd healed me once. Slowly stitched me back together.

I'd grown a lot since then. Learned to love myself and feel confident in my own skin.

But he'd been there. Every step of the way, Kaiden was right beside me. And I worried that without him, it would all come crumbling down.

"Hi," I said, smiling up at him.

He banded his arms around me, drawing me close. "Hi."

Leaning down, he brushed his nose along my cheek before stealing a chaste kiss.

"God, I'm going to miss you," he said, his voice cracking a little.

"I'll miss you too."

So much.

I anchored my hands around the back of his neck and held on for dear life.

Because the truth was, I never wanted to let go.

CHAPTER TEN

KAIDEN

FUCK, this was harder than I thought it would be.

I was on the precipice of everything I'd ever wanted but I hadn't ever imagined it would feel like I was giving up a part of my soul.

It was a temporary separation. One summer. That was all and yet... Why did it feel like time was running out?

Why did it feel like goodbye?

It wasn't, I knew that really. But it didn't stop my mind from working overtime.

I should have asked her already.

I almost had earlier when she was curled up beside me. But I'd stopped myself.

It didn't feel right to do it now. Tonight. Not when come the morning, I would have to leave.

Didn't stop me feeling like I'd royally fucked things up though.

"You're so fucking beautiful," I said, brushing my knuckles down Lily's cheek. She inhaled a shuddering breath as her lashes fluttered. "I'm going to strip you naked now and worship every inch of you, okay?"

"Mm-hmm," she murmured, heat spilling into her cheeks.

Winding my hand in the back of her hair, I titled her face up and ran my tongue over the seam of Lily's lips.

I'd had almost five years to learn her body. Her likes and dislikes. Lily was no longer the shy uncertain girl I'd kissed in the Filmers' boat shed but she still retreated into herself sometimes.

But I liked that. *Loved* that about her. I loved that sometimes I had to work for it. For the chance to see her come undone.

With steady hands, I stripped her naked, feasting on the tempting curves of her body.

It was Lily.

It had been her since senior year and it would always be her. No matter what happened in the next few weeks nothing would change that.

Lily helped me get my own clothes off. My t-shirt. My sweatpants and boxers. Until we were skin on skin, my hands mapping the swell of her hips, the dip of her spine.

"Love you, Lil," I said, gazing down at her.

"I love you too." She smiled and this one felt full of love and understanding.

Scooping Lily up into my arms, her laughter filled the room as I carried her over to the bed. "God, you get me so hard," I rasped, falling down on top of her.

"Kaiden," she whimpered, her legs falling open to accommodate me.

I ran one hand down her body and kissed her. Slow and deep, tangling my tongue with hers. My body vibrated with need, but I wanted to take my time. Memorize every touch, every sigh and moan.

"Are you wet for me, Lily?" I dipped my fingers between our bodies, finding her pussy. A groan of approval rumbled in my chest. She was soaked. "Tell me when it feels good," I whispered the words onto her lips as I pressed two fingers into her.

"God," she breathed, arching into my touch.

"You like it?"

Lily nodded, her lip parted on a soft sigh. "More."

"You want more, babe? Like this?" I curled my

fingers deep, rubbing that spot inside her that made everything intense.

"Yes, God yes." She curled her hand over my shoulder, dragging me closer. "It always feels so good."

"You going to come for me like a good girl?" I asked, earning me another whimper. "That's it, ride my hand, Lil."

She did, rocking her body against me, taking what she needed. I added a third finger, stretching her, all while tasting the skin at her throat. Sucking and licking, driving her wild.

"Kaiden... God, it feels so good."

"Come for me, babe. Come all over my fingers."

Her entire body went tight, her little whimpers like music to my ears. And when she shattered, it was so fucking beautiful.

"Yes... yes," she cried, her thighs clenched around my hand.

I kissed her through the pleasure, stroking her tongue with my own. I was rock-hard and desperate to be inside her but I lived for this—for making my shy, reserved girl come apart.

"Fuck, I'm going to miss this," I said, taking myself in my hand and nudging up against her slick core.

"Shh." Lily kissed me, hitching her legs around my waist and I buried myself inside her.

"You are perfect," I groaned. "My perfect girl. I love you." *So fucking much.*

"I love you too." She wrapped her arms around my shoulders, anchoring us together. It was intense like this, slow and deep and intimate. But we needed this.

I needed it.

"Ah," she breathed as I rocked forward, filling her to the hilt. Her eyelids fluttered shut, but I gently closed my fingers around her throat, desperate for the connection.

"Look at me, Lil. I need to see your eyes." To know she was here with me. Today. Tomorrow. Eight weeks from now.

Next year…

Forever.

"Kaiden?" She gazed up at me with confusion.

I hadn't realized I'd stopped, lost to the thoughts running through my mind.

The regrets.

"What's wrong?" She laid her hand on my cheek, the confusion glittering in her eyes giving way to concern.

"Me and you, Lil. Always."

"Always." She kissed me hard, distracting me with her luscious lips and perfect body.

But despite losing myself in the taste of her, the very feel of her wrapped around me, I'd seen the fear in her eyes, the flash of vulnerability.

The uncertainty.

That was okay though. I'd be strong enough for both of us. Lily Ford was mine.

And I'd find a way to remind her that every single day I was gone.

POPPY

"Lily, it's me." I opened her bedroom door a fraction and poked my head inside. "Can I come in?"

Her hand shot up out of the pile of cushions and blankets and she beckoned me inside.

"Seriously, it's like eighty degrees out."

"I'm wallowing."

"Oh, Lil." Climbing on the bed beside her, I snuggled up close. "It's only a few weeks."

"It feels like forever."

"It's one summer. And you have so much to look forward to. The baby is here. Avery's wedding is in a couple of weeks. There's the bachelorette party. Hanging with your friends, your sister"—I nudged her arm—"it'll fly by, you'll see."

"When did you get back?" she asked, ignoring my attempt to cheer her up.

"Ten minutes ago. I literally dumped my bags and came to find you."

"I'm glad you're here."

"Me too, Lilster. Me too." Comfortable silence fell over us. Until I said, "Have you heard from him?"

Kaiden had been gone a day and half and according to Mom, Lily wasn't handling it well. But I was here now, and I'd find a way to distract her from her negative feelings.

"He called me this morning before practice."

"And…"

"He's fine."

"And…"

"He misses me already."

"Of course he does." I hugged her tighter. "Football is Kaiden's soul food. But you're his lighthouse, babe. You'll always guide him home." She glanced back at me, and I frowned. "What?"

"That was a little weird."

"Hush," I scoffed, "you know what I mean. Besides, Lily Lighthouse has a nice ring to it."

"You're such a goofball. Where's Aaron?"

"He went home to see his parents. We're going to alternate between the Bennets' house and here. It'll be nice to spend some time together."

She laced her hands over my arm and squeezed. "I'm glad you're here."

"Me too. But enough with the wallowing, okay? Kaiden is off chasing his dream. He's not dead."

Lily rolled over and glowered at me. "That isn't funny."

"It wasn't supposed to be. It's okay to be sad, Lil. But in a few weeks, you'll be reunited, and you know what they say about some time apart..." She stared at me expectantly, and I grinned. "Epic reunion sex."

"Poppy!"

"Oh, relax. You're not a shy meek eighteen-year-old anymore, babe. You're a fierce twenty-two-year-old woman. You've got this. Now tell me all about baby River."

We both lay on our backs, staring up at the ceiling as Lily described the newest member of our family. "She's so tiny, Poppy. Peyton is terrified."

"Understandable. But Mom said the doctors are pleased with her progress."

"Yeah, she's doing really well all things considered."

"I still can't believe Peyton had a child with Xander," I said.

"They've been together for four years."

"I know but it's Xander."

"You should have seen him. He looked at Peyton like she was his everything."

"I can't wait to go see them. I think we're going to try and visit tomorrow if you want to come."

"Yeah, maybe."

"Got other plans?"

"No, but—"

"You're coming."

"Fine." She huffed, and I chuckled.

"We're going to have an amazing summer, Lil. You'll see."

She didn't answer but one way or another, I'd make sure of it.

"Hey, sweetie, come in. Aaron and his dad are in the yard."

"Thanks, Mya," I said, hugging her.

"I'm so happy to have you both home. How's Lily? Aaron said you went to see her."

"She's... Lily. Hopefully in a couple of days, she'll feel better. We're going to see Peyton, Xander, and the baby tomorrow."

"Oh, that'll do her good. Your mom said they're doing good with all things considering the situation."

"They are. I think they're talking about sending Peyton home after the weekend. But I'm not sure she'll want to leave River."

"Hopefully, they can figure something out. Come on, let's grab some drinks and head outside."

"Sure." I followed her through their beautiful home. It was almost as familiar as my own house, a core memory of growing up in Rixon. Probably something to do with the fact that I'd loved their son for as long as I could remember.

My heart fluttered. There had been a time I thought we would never figure out our shit. But we had, and almost four years later, I got to spend every day loving my best friend.

Life was good.

Great, even.

And despite my sister's mood, and Peyton's baby surprise, I was determined to enjoy the summer.

"There she is," Asher called the second we stepped into the yard. "Hey, Poppy, good to see you," he added.

Aaron got straight up and stalked over, pulling me into arms.

"Babe," I warned, aware of his parents sitting right there.

But he didn't care, he never did.

It was one of the things I loved most about him, that he wasn't scared to show the world he loved me.

"Mmm, missed you." His lips brushed over mine.

"It's barely been three hours."

"Three hours too long," he murmured.

"Put the girl down, Son. You've spent an entire year playing house with her. It's our time now."

Soft laughter spilled out of me as I buried my face in his neck, breathing him in.

"Like you and Mom are any better," Aaron shot back.

"Damn, he's got me there." Asher pulled his wife in for a kiss.

"Ash," Mya shoved him away. "Behave."

"The kids return and suddenly I'm pushed to the bottom of the pile." He pouted, all puppy dog eyes and dejection.

I'd seen that face so many times. It was the same one Aaron used on me when he couldn't get his own way. Usually with whatever new sexual experiment he wanted to try.

My beau was insatiable.

"Come on, Mom made tacos." Aaron led me over to the outdoor sectional and we sat down.

"I hope you've been keeping my son in line, Poppy." Asher smiled.

"I try my best."

"Atta girl. Last summer before senior year. Makes me feel as old as shit."

"Ash, we're in our late forties, it's hardly ancient."

"I know but it just feels significant. Before we know it, the kids will be done with college. They'll be getting married and having kids of their own. We'll be grandparents, babe. Grand. Parents. I'm not ready for that."

"Good thing, Dad, because we're not thinking about any of that any time soon." Aaron gazed down at me, a knowing twinkle in his.

We talked about the future, sure. But we were content with living in the now, soaking up college life, and learning who we were. Who we wanted to be.

I didn't need a grand declaration to know I was his and he was mine. It just was.

And always would be.

CHAPTER ELEVEN

KAIDEN

"OKAY, GUYS, BRING IT IN," Coach McElroy yelled across the field.

"Thank fuck," Forest, a running back from Philly, grumbled. "If I have to run one more drill, I swear, my legs are gonna fall off."

"Suck it up, brother." Another rookie, a guy named Jay, clapped him on the back. "It's only day four and we spent two of those in the classroom. We got a whole summer of drills yet." His gaze landed on me. "Good game out there, Thatcher."

"Thanks." I grabbed a water bottle out of the caddy and joined the rest of the guys in the huddle.

Since arriving at the facility, it had been a whirlwind of information, study time, practices, meetings with the coaching staff, and getting to know my fellow rookies.

I'd barely had time to catch my breath, let alone call Lily.

We texted every day, and I'd managed to video call her for ten minutes last night before the guys burst into my room, demanding we bond.

It would settle down soon enough though. At least, I hoped it would. Besides, from what I could tell Poppy was keeping her busy enough. And she had Peyton and the baby to fuss over.

"I'm impressed with what I've seen today," Coach said. "You took your learning and applied it to the game. Thatcher, you showed strong leadership out there today. Well done."

I gave him an appreciative nod, aware of the rest of the guys looking at me, wearing a mix of jealousy, respect, and support.

Right now, these guys were my friends, my teammates, but the harsh reality was we wouldn't all make the cut. And I wanted it.

Fuck, I wanted it.

The Wild's roster was full of senior players. Their QB wasn't getting any younger and rumor was they were keen to bring through the younger players. But they'd drafted two of us this year. Me and a guy out of Fitton U, up in Ohio. He was good but I was better.

And if only one of us made the cut, I intended on making damn sure it was me.

"Tomorrow, we're going to start working through the plays," the first-year coach said. "Getting you up to speed with the playbook. I suggest you all take some time to study tonight. Okay, hit the showers. We'll see you bright and early."

I doused myself with the rest of my water, grateful for the burst of cold trickling over my face and down the back of my neck. It had been a grueling day under the sun and my skin had a slight crisp to it.

"He's right, you know," Forest said, jogging up beside me. "You looked good out there."

"You didn't do so bad yourself."

"You want to hang tonight? Go over the playbook?"

"Sure. But let's keep it low-key."

I really wanted to carve out some time to talk to Lily and I didn't feel like being sociable.

"Sounds good to me. Meet at my room or yours?"

"I'll come to you," I said.

The team had taken over a floor in an upscale hotel downtown, and we'd all been assigned a roommate for the duration. I was bunking with first-round pick, linebacker Chad Michelson. A big, brawny guy who kicked ass on the field but preferred to keep to himself off of it.

I headed into the locker room. Everything still felt strange as fuck. Unfamiliar faces, new personalities, a strange new environment.

I'd known coming into camp that it would be tough, but nothing could have prepared me for how intense it would be. This time together was devised to keep our focus solely on football. No family visits, no fucking around, and barely any downtime.

For the next few weeks, we'd eat, breathe, and live football. But if you wanted to be the best, you had to earn it. You had to show up, leave your ego at the door, and work for it. Every. Single. Day.

There wasn't a single part of me that didn't ache as I stripped out of my gear and headed to the showers. The blast of hot water went some way to smoothing out the knots in my muscles, but I was used to a little pain after a hard day's training.

At college, Lily often gave me a massage, working the kinks out with her delicate fingers and her favorite body lotion.

Fuck, I missed her.

Four days.

Not even a week, and I was already craving her. And it wasn't even the physical stuff. It was just her. Her light. Her presence. The way she grounded me.

I'd spent four years with Lily, laughing and living and loving, so to suddenly not have her close by was strange. She'd always been my anchor so without her, it felt a little like trying to stay afloat in stormy seas.

Or maybe that was just the ten hours out on the field in the early summer heat talking.

When I was done washing the day's sweat and grime off my body, I grabbed a towel and rubbed down, before pulling it tight around my hips.

A couple of the guys' wolf-whistled as I made my way back to my locker.

The Wild's facility was something else, and the thought of this place being my home for the foreseeable future lit a fire in my chest.

I wanted it.

I wanted it so fucking much.

I just had to put in the work, impress the coaching staff, and hold myself together for the next few weeks.

> Lily: I'll call you as soon as I leave xo

> Kaiden: Okay, I can't wait to see you. We should get some time tonight.

> Lily: Sounds good. It's going okay, though?

> Kaiden: It's intense. But we knew it would be. Coach noticed me today.

> Lily: Of course he did. I miss you xo

> Kaiden: Miss you too. Call me as soon as you can. I'm heading over to Forest's room to chill but I'll be waiting.

> Lily: Okay xo

I pocketed my cell and grabbed my copy of the team's playbook. I'd already read the thing once cover to cover but it was going to take time to absorb everything.

"I'm heading out," I said to Chad.

"Sure thing." He didn't lift his head up from whatever had his attention on his phone.

"Okay, then," I murmured, slipping into the hall.

Forest was only a few doors down. I knocked and waited for him to answer.

"Thought you'd stood me up," he said the second the door swung open.

"Sorry, I was texting Lily."

"How's that going?"

"That?" I arched a brow.

"Yeah, you know what they say. Happy wife, happy life."

"She's not..."

"Same thing." He shrugged, beckoning me inside.

"It's only been a few days."

"Women are a distraction, man."

"We should study," I said.

I wasn't here to dissect my relationship with Lily. As far as I was concerned, that was non-negotiable. Did it suck we would spend most of the summer apart? Hell, yes. But once training camp was out of the way, and Lily got settled in Kansas, we would be together again, and things would all work out.

She had a couple of leads for a job but there was no rush. My signing bonus alone would cover us for as long as we needed. But Lily had dreams of her own to chase, and I would always support her.

"Straight down to business," Forest snorted, "I like your style."

"Where's your roommate?" I asked.

"A few of the guys headed down to the games room I think."

I nodded, flipping open the playbook. It was a

strange thing to be starting over. Four year's worth of plays, of knowing my teammates strengths and weaknesses, of commanding them, only to be back at square one.

But Forest was good people, and only a couple of days in we already worked well together.

"So what do you make of things so far?" he asked. "Is it what you expected?"

"I'm not sure anyone can know what to expect when you get the call up," I replied.

"True. I knew it would be tough, I didn't realize they'd have us on lockdown."

"Makes sense. They want us to be one hundred percent focused on the team."

"No distractions. No drama," he echoed Coach McElroy's words from our first day at camp.

"Feels weird that we won't all make the cut."

"Not us, man. We're gonna make it." Forest smirked, flipping through the playbook.

"I hope you're right."

Because I didn't come here only to fail at the last hurdle.

I came here to win.

To make it.

To earn myself a spot on the team.

Anything else, simply wasn't an option.

LILY

"Where are you?" I muttered as the call rang out again.

Three times, I'd called Kaiden. It wasn't late. Later than I'd planned, sure. But he surely wouldn't be sleeping yet.

I pulled up our chat and typed a quick message.

> Lily: Hey, it's me. I keep calling but it just rings out. Let me know when's a good time. Can't wait to talk to you xo

He wouldn't stand me up. Not after telling me that he would make time to call tonight. Except, after another thirty minutes had passed, it was obvious that's exactly what he'd done.

Tears pricked my eyes as I stared at my phone, wishing it to ring.

It had only been four days, but it felt like forever. Kaiden was such a big part of my life to suddenly not have him there was a lot to deal with.

> Lily: I guess you're busy. I'm going to bed. Talk tomorrow.

A rogue tear slipped free. God, I felt stupid, getting upset so soon. But I couldn't help it.

I couldn't pretend that it didn't worry me that I would have to compete with football now that he'd been drafted.

I wanted to be more secure and confident in myself and our relationship, but everything was changing. Moving without me.

At least, that's what it felt like.

Shaking off the depressing thoughts, I cleaned up for bed and climbed under my covers, checking my phone one last time. But there was still nothing.

Kaiden didn't text.

And I spent most of the night awake, wondering if things were ever going to be how they used to be.

I woke to a brass band in my head.

I'd tossed and turned half the night, and maybe checked my cell phone once or twice.

A groan slipped free when I realized it was still early. Too early for someone who had barely slept. But when I reached for my cell and saw Kaiden's name, my mood instantly improved. Sitting up a little, I opened his messages and smiled.

> Kaiden: Shit, Lil. I am so sorry. I went back to my room and crashed. I woke up fully dressed with the playbook stuck to my face. Forgive me? I love you xo

> Lily: Of course I forgive you. I'm sorry it took so long. Mom and Aunt Hailee are taking their bachelorette party responsibilities very seriously. Give me five and I'll call xo

But when I got done quickly peeing and brushing my teeth, Kaiden's phone rang out again.

He must have already started practice.

Frustration welled inside me. I just wanted to hear his voice. To talk to him.

To soothe the ache in my heart.

I guess I'd have to wait though, and only hope he found time to call me later.

CHAPTER TWELVE

COLE

"SHH, YOU GOTTA BE QUIET." I nipped the inside of Sofia's thigh, one hand pressed over her mouth as she writhed beneath me.

"Too good," she quietly murmured, lifting her hips, seeking more.

I grinned, reveling in how easily she begged for me.

Teasing her was one of my favorite pastimes. Since we stayed in Vera a lot, and there wasn't a lot of room, we had to get creative. So waking up in her bed this morning was a luxury I didn't plan on wasting.

The only problem was my girl was a screamer. And the last thing I wanted was her parents to overhear my early morning wake up call.

Sofia's fingers slid into my hair as she tried to take control.

"Patience," I chided, smirking against her hip bone as I trailed a path down her silky skin.

"Cole, stop teasing me..."

"But it's so much fun."

The second I put my mouth on her, she gasped, fingers digging into my scalp as I sucked her clit.

"Yes, yes... yes," she cried, the little moans drowned out by my palm.

"Quiet."

But I didn't mean it, not really. I loved hearing her come apart, moan my name, and beg for more. It was moments like these that reminded me she was here. Healthy and happy and alive.

Of course, I liked the moments where we were doing all the mundane things too, but there was nothing better than her taste on my tongue and my name on her lips.

"Cole, more..." She held me closer, forcing my head right where she wanted it.

This time, I let her. Because it was all for her, always.

If being with Sofia had taught me anything, it was that life was short—too fucking short. Tomorrow was never guaranteed. You had to make every moment count and I liked to think we'd done plenty of that in the last three years.

But it didn't stop the fear from taking hold occasionally. The knowledge that one day, the cancer could come back. That I might lose her.

Some days, I wondered if I should put a ring on her finger and baby inside her. But I had to believe we had time.

I had to believe that we had a lifetime ahead of us.

Anything else was too fucking terrifying.

"Hey." She stroked her thumb along the back of my ear. "Where'd you go just now?"

"Nowhere." I tried to lock down those unwanted thoughts and focus on the present. But Sofia knew.

She always knew.

"Come here." She gently tugged me up her body until I was pressed up against her. "I'm here, Cole," she said. "I'm not going anywhere."

"I know." I touched my head to hers and breathed in deeply.

"I'm sorry. I don't know what came over me."

"It's okay. It hits me too sometimes." She laid her hand on my cheek. "I love you."

"I love you too, so fucking much."

"Yeah?" Love and lust glittered in her eyes. "Feel

like showing me then? Because I was so close just then..."

"Shit, babe. I'm a bad boyfriend." I went to move down her body to finish the job, but she stopped me.

"I want you, Cole. I want you to fuck me."

"Babe," I groaned, loving how dirty the words sounded rolling off her tongue.

"Please."

Who was I to deny her?

I'd give this girl the world if I could. But I hoped she was satisfied with our simple but fulfilled life. Traveling. Art and music. Helping other kids less fortunate than us.

It should have been no surprise that Sofia had an open heart and a kind soul. She was a Bennet, after all. But the fact she knew how precious life was only made all that shine brighter.

"You, Sofia Bennet, can have anything you want." I kissed her as I slowly rocked forward, filling her to the hilt.

She moaned against my lips, hitching her legs around my waist and rocking her body with mine. "I'll never grow tired of this, of you." She stared at me with such intensity, I felt sucker punched.

"Good thing then," I whispered, kissing her again. Harder. Deeper. Mimicking the way I rode her body.

Because I had zero plans of ever letting her go.

SOFIA

"Good morning, sweetheart," Dad said as I entered the kitchen. "Sleep well?"

There was that usual teasing lilt in his voice. The one that made me squirm and blush no matter how many times I heard it.

Nobody liked thinking about their parents having sex or their parents referencing you having sex. But that was my dad. Asher Bennet romantic at heart and perpetual tease.

"I did actually," I said, trying to keep a straight face.

"I'm sure you did."

"Ash," Mom appeared with the laundry basket in her hands.

"What? It's just a question, babe. A nice, normal quest—"

"Morning." Cole strolled in, looking every bit the rock star he could have been.

God, he looked good. Damp tousled dark hair. A black fitted t-shirt that revealed his tan muscular arms. The tattoo that snaked up his bicep. I still couldn't quite believe he was mine.

The boy who had stood by me through the hardest few months of my life was all man now.

And my father was looking at him like he knew exactly what we had been up to this morning.

God help me.

"Cole, son. Good sleep?"

"Dad!" My cheeks burned. "Do you have to be so weird?"

Mom chuckled. "Don't mind your father, sweetheart. There's coffee in the pot, Cole. Help yourself."

"Thanks, Mrs. B."

My boyfriend came and wrapped his arm around my waist, dropping a kiss on my head. "You want?"

"Yes, please."

Cole headed over to the counter and I looked up to find my dad watching me.

"What?"

"Makes me happy seeing you happy, or is that a crime too?" Amusement danced in his eyes, but his voice was thick with emotion.

"Don't go getting all sappy on me," I warned. "Mom, tell him."

"Hey, I'm allowed to get all up in my feelings. You know, you and Aaron should count your lucky stars that you got me as your old man and not Jase."

"Jase is cool," I said.

"Cool?" He scoffed. "He's not cooler than me."

"I don't know, Mr. B."

"Cole, we've talked about this, son. It's been years. If you care about my fragile ego at all, you'll call me Ash."

"Sure thing, Mr. B." Cole shot me a knowing grin while he made our coffees.

"You know, son," Dad got up. "It's a good thing I like you. You two behave while we're gone. No funny business—"

"Dad!"

"Just keeping things real." He waggled his brows. "You might be Cole's girl, but you'll always be my little girl. I'll catch you kids later. Some of us have to work."

"Hey, we work," I called after him. But I knew he was only joking. He and Mom supported me one hundred percent.

"What's the plan today?" Mom asked.

"I have a full day of lessons," Cole said.

"And me and the girls are taking Lily out. She's feeling a little down since Kaiden left."

"Yeah, it can't be easy. But it isn't forever."

"I still can't believe he made it." I arched a brow as if to say really, and Cole chuckled. "I mean, I can totally believe it. It's Thatcher. If anyone was going to go all the way, it was him. But it's the NFL. It doesn't get any better than that."

"He's still the same person."

"Yeah, now. But wait until the season starts. His life will never be the same again."

"Oh, I don't know." I shrugged. "He'll always be just Kaiden to me."

He had a good head on his shoulders and didn't seem like the kind of guy to forget where he came from. Besides, Lily would keep him grounded. I knew she was worried now but once things settled down and she joined him in Kansas, everything would work itself out.

"All I'm saying is, I hope he can get us some good tickets for the opening game."

I rolled my eyes at Cole.

"Have you girls got anything special planned?" Mom asked.

"Actually, I think they're all coming here. We were thinking of hanging out by the pool."

"Sounds good. Just make sure you apply enough lotion. It's going to be a hot one."

"I will, Mom." I smiled. Even at the tender age of twenty-one, I was still her baby.

She left me and Cole alone, and he wasted no time in coming over to cage me in against the breakfast counter.

"Mmm, good morning." He kissed me.

"It was." I smirked. "Until I came down and my dad had to make it obvious he knew exactly what we were up to."

"He doesn't care, babe. All he cares about is that his baby girl is happy. And from what I can remember, you were very, very happy this morning."

"Cole," I breathed, hardly able to think straight with him so close.

"Yeah, Sofe?" My name seemed to dangle. He knew exactly what he was doing, and I was powerless to stop it.

"I love you," I said, hoping to distract him.

"Hmm, I see what you did there." He pulled back, grinning.

"We don't need to give my dad more reason to tease us." I pointed out.

"This is true. Although I'm pretty sure, he's caught Aaron and Poppy at it way more than us."

"Okay, that's... weird. I do not want to think about my brother and best friend having sex. Like ever." My nose crinkled.

"Honestly, I'm a little surprised he hasn't put a baby inside her yet with the amount those two go at it."

"I love my brother and I can't wait to be an aunt

one day but not yet. Not for at least another five or six years."

"So you don't want a little me or you running around the place?"

"One day, yes. All the yeses. But not yet." I slung my arms over his shoulders. "I want to live, Cole. I want to have adventures and see the world."

"You know I'll follow you anywhere, right?"

"To the ends of the Earth?"

"And over the edge so long as we're together."

My heart swelled at his words. "You know, you really are romantic when you want to be."

"If it means I get to keep you," he kissed the end of my nose. "I can live with that."

CHAPTER THIRTEEN

LILY

"HAVE YOU TALKED TO HIM YET?" Poppy asked me as we sipped our mimosas.

Avery and Miley had arrived yesterday afternoon, so Aunt Hailee, Mom, and Mrs. Fuller were in full wedding mode.

Today, it was a pre-bachelorette party pamper session. Then on the weekend, it was the actual bachelorette party.

"We've texted."

"And..."

"I already told you, he apologized, sent me some flowers, and I got over it."

"Oh, you sound so over it." She grinned, poking her tongue out at me.

I waved her off, not liking the fact that she was right.

I wasn't over it.

But there wasn't much I could do about it. Kaiden was knee deep in training camp. He didn't have time to worry about anything else. And I didn't want to be a distraction. He'd worked too hard to ruin his shot at this all because his needy girlfriend couldn't get her shit together.

God, mental health really sucked sometimes. I could be my biggest cheerleader... and my worst critic. It was exhausting.

There was no time to wallow today though. Because this was Miley's moment, everything else needed to take a back seat.

"It's a shame Peyton couldn't be here," she said, positively glowing thanks to all the sunshine we'd been having and her upcoming nuptials to my cousin.

"How is she, really?"

"She'll get there," I said.

Things were hard still but it was early days. River was growing stronger every day but Peyton was struggling. So much so, Xander had taken extended leave to stay with her.

"How are you feeling about the big day?" Poppy asked.

"Nervous. But everything has been checked and double checked."

"And triple checked." Miley's mom sang. "Everything is going to be perfect, sweetheart. And your dress, perfection. Avery won't know what hit him."

"I'm so happy for you both," I said.

"Thanks. It feels like it's been a long time coming, you know."

We all nodded, well aware that it had been almost five years since he'd popped the question. But after Avery was drafted to the Steelers, their plans took a little detour.

Football hadn't gotten into the way for them though, it had only delayed things a while.

"And we have the bachelorette party to look forward to," Mom added.

They all started to discuss the weekend's plans, but my mind was stuck on Kaiden. On the fact that we'd barely spoken since the other night.

I didn't want to worry everyone with it, so I'd pasted on a smile and told everyone I was fine.

I didn't feel fine though. I felt like my carefully constructed world was slowly crumbling around me.

I knew it wasn't healthy to be so dependent on someone. But Kaiden was my anchor. He had been ever since senior year. He grounded me in a way nothing had ever managed to before, and while I wasn't pulling my hair again—I hadn't done that for a long time now—those familiar urges were rumbling inside me. So much so I'd almost added a scrunchie to my wrist this morning.

"It's a shame Kaiden isn't going to make it to the bachelor party."

"Yeah," I said, aware that they were all watching me.

"At least he'll be here for the wedding," Poppy quickly added, offering me a reassuring smile.

"Of course he'll be here for the wedding," Mom said. "He knows how important it is to Lily."

Poppy, Ashleigh, and I were bridesmaids along with Miley's best friend Tara.

Aaron, Cole, Ezra, and Kaiden were groomsmen and Tara's partner Flint, Avery's best friend, was best man.

I had been looking forward to it, but that was before everything started to implode.

Not everything, me.

I knew couples went through highs and lows, especially high school sweethearts. Life was paved with big decisions and hard times. I also knew people thought I should feel lucky to be with one of the top picks in this year's draft, but I couldn't change who I was. I could only continue to battle my demons and try to keep my worries at bay. And remind myself that Kaiden loved me. Football—a contract with one of the top teams in the country—didn't change that.

"Okay," Mrs. Fuller chirped. "Who wants more mimosas?"

"Mom!" Miley gawked. "It's not supposed to be that kind of afternoon."

"Oh hush, sweetheart. We're celebrating. My baby is getting married."

"Someone take the champagne off the crazy lady," Miley murmured with a smile.

Everyone let her mom fill their glasses except Miley.

Strange.

She noticed me watching and sent me a soft smile.

Oh my God.

She was pregnant. I don't know how I hadn't noticed it sooner. We'd all had at least two mimosas, but Miley was still nursing her one glass. In fact, it was barely touched.

Giving an imperceptible shake of her head, she silently begged me not to reveal her secret. I gave her a small nod.

A strange mix of happiness and jealousy surged through me.

I wanted that.

I wanted the white wedding and babies. But if everything went to plan, my boyfriend was about to become one of the most famous NFL players in history.

He would belong to the franchise. The fans.

Football.

It had always owned a piece of him, but I'd never felt secondary to the game.

Until now.

AARON

"You think you're ready?"

"Ready?" Avery frowned at me as we tossed a ball around in the pool.

"Yeah, man. To tie the knot."

"I've been ready since the day I put a ring on her finger."

"Don't give him any ideas," Ezra smirked, and I flipped him off.

"Like you aren't planning on putting a ring on Leigh Leigh's finger."

"Nah, there's no rush," he said. But I saw the glint of want in his eyes. The yearning.

Of course, he planned on putting a ring on it. He was as all-in as the rest of us.

"What's stopping you?" Avery arched his brow,

flicking his eyes over to where Jase and my dad were shooting the shit. His lips curved with amusement, and I rolled my eyes.

"I am not scared of Jason."

"Keep telling yourself that, brother." Laughter rumbled in Ezra's chest.

"Fuck you, man. Fuck. You. I'll pop the question when I'm good and ready."

"I always thought Kaiden would be the first one to do it," Avery said.

"Yeah. Feels weird as shit he's not here," Gav added. "But you'd know all about that, Chase."

"It'll calm down. Rookie camp is no joke."

"Yeah, from what Poppy said, he's hardly been in touch with Lily."

"It's intense. The coaches want you focused on nothing but the team. But he'll come out the other side."

"Wearing a Wild jersey," Bryan grinned.

"If anyone can earn his spot, it's Kaiden."

"Burgers are ready," Dad called, and we all piled out of the pool, grabbing our towels.

"This was a good call," Jase said as we joined them over at the table.

"Barbecue, beer, and the sunshine, what more could a guy want?" Cameron added. "Just don't get sunburnt, Son. You don't want to ruin your wedding photos with a shiny face."

"Relax, Dad, I applied lotion." Avery shook his head.

"Okay, dig in." Dad slid a plate of patties onto the table. "Just don't tell your mom there wasn't any healthy options in sight."

"Mya got you on a diet again, Mr. B?" Avery asked.

"Something like that. I love that woman beyond words, but she drives me crazy. If it's not a diet, it's a new supplement or exercise."

"She has a point, Ash. You have gained a little weight." Jase said, barely containing his laughter.

"I'm barely five pounds heavier than I was five years ago."

"He's just messing with you, old man," I said.

"Old man, huh? You want to put that to the test, *Son*?"

"Let's eat," Cam intervened, knowing that the two of us could be as competitive as hell once we got going.

I loved my dad, loved him something fierce. But we didn't always see eye to eye.

He wanted me to have a better plan for after college. I wanted to enjoy my last year before I had to go out into the real world. Thankfully, Poppy was all too happy to roll with the punches and see where things took us.

Despite a successful three years with the Rams, football wasn't in my future. Just as gymnastics wasn't in Poppy's.

But we would both have our degrees and the fortunate positions to come home to Rixon and figure out the next chapter of our lives.

"I wonder what the women are up to?" Dad said.

"Sipping mimosas, getting mani-pedis and talking about us, no doubt," Jase huffed. "I still don't see why we can't have one big bachelor/bachelorette party."

"One word Jase," Mr. Fuller cleared his throat, looking a strange mix of excitement and uncertainty. "Strippers."

"Ted, come on... I thought we agreed."

"Son, what happens at the bachelor party, stays at the bachelor party." He winked, and my dad, Jase, and Asher laughed.

Avery wasn't laughing though.

"Just roll with it," I said. "It's not like we don't all know Miley has you by the balls."

"Yeah, and I happen to like them attached to my body. No fucking strip clubs."

"You say that now, but once the liquor is flowing..." Ezra shrugged.

"Seriously, you're all okay with this?"

"I'm not against it." Gav said. "I mean, for research purposes only."

"You know who would be against it, Kaiden," Avery grumbled. "And the motherfucker won't even be here."

"How about we set a rule: no private dances or lap dances," Bryan suggested.

"Come on, Cole? Help a guy out."

"Don't look at me." He held up his hands. "I'll go with the flow."

"You suck. You all royally suck." Avery huffed. "Haven't you seen The Hangover? That's a warning to every bachelor party out there."

"Oh yeah, because a round of golf and drinks will get wild," I chuckled. "Hold up, so you're saying you've never been to a strip club before?"

"No," he grimaced, "I'm saying I don't want to go again. Miley will lose her shit if she finds out."

"Like the girls won't be getting her some Magic Mike wannabe stripper."

"They wouldn't—"

"Of course they would. Poppy is involved in the planning," Cole chuckled, and I flipped him off.

But he had a point. My girl could get a little wild, especially if there was champagne involved.

That's not to say I didn't trust her one hundred

percent, I did. But my girl liked to party, and she liked to cause a little mischief occasionally. Something I regularly benefited from.

A smile ghosted my lips remembering her latest mission—exploring tantric sex. I wasn't complaining, it was some of the best damn sex of my life, but it had lasted hours. To the point where I thought she was going to kill me.

Death by orgasm.

What a way to go.

I chuckled to myself and the guys all gawked at me. "What?" I played dumb.

"Okay, everyone." Cameron stood, a beer in his hand. "I just wanted to say a few words. Son, I'm proud of the man you've become, the husband I know you'll be to Miley. She's the perfect woman to complement you and remind you that despite what Jase might say, there is more to life than football. There's family. So enjoy the burgers and beer. Enjoy your weekend. But then remember one thing. Once you say 'I do,' she owns your ass."

Laughter rang out around the yard.

"Some men spend their entire lives running from commitment. But that's not who we are. You're a Chase, Son. And when we find someone worth loving, we do it with every piece of ourselves. To Avery and Miley." Cam lifted his beer high and locked eyes with his son. "May your future be full of love and laughter and lots and lots of—"

"Kinky sex," Dad grinned like a fool.

"Jesus, Ash. A little decorum. Sorry, Ted. He doesn't get out much."

"Oh, it's okay, Cam." Miley's dad smiled. "He's only saying what we're all thinking."

"Actually, I'm thinking marriage is a sex killer," Jase grumbled. "In fact," he pinned me with a dark look and then said nine little words that made my stomach drop. "Why haven't you put a ring on it yet?"

"Uh, I..." I stuttered, unable to find my voice.

"Hmm, I'm watching you, Bennet." Jase glowered, and I sank into my seat a little.

I loved the man like family but, Jesus, he knew how to make a guy squirm.

Ezra leaned over and whispered, "See, that was practically his blessing. So what are you waiting for?"

I guess he had a point.

CHAPTER FOURTEEN

KAIDEN

FOOTBALL HAD ALWAYS BEEN my dream. It was my first love. My passion. Pretty sure it was part of my DNA by now.

But rookie camp took things to a whole new level.

One I wasn't entirely sure I was prepared for.

Almost a week in, and I was exhausted. And not just the kind of exhausted you experienced after a tough game or a long run first thing in the morning, but the kind of exhausted you felt all the way down to your bones.

The coaching staff didn't let up. They constantly demanded more. More drills. More plays. More effort.

A couple of the guys had already left. One through choice and one because of injury.

But I hadn't come all this way not to find myself on the bench in a Wild jersey come the new season.

Still, being here without Lily was an added level of torture I had to endure.

She was still pissed at me for missing our phone call earlier in the week. But our schedules never aligned. She had shit going on with the wedding plans and Peyton and the baby. And I had ten-hour practices that felt like they might never end.

I was hoping to make it to the wedding in a week's time though. We had a scheduled weekend off before regular camp started.

The test would really come then, once the rest of the senior players arrived, ready to size up the fresh meat as we'd been referred to a lot over the last seven days.

Head Coach McElroy, and the offensive coach coordinator seemed to be impressed with my performance, but they weren't giving much away, so I didn't want to assume I would make the roster.

My phone vibrated and I plucked it off the table. Lunch was one of the short windows in the day we had to check for messages and contact home. But disappointment welled in my chest when I realized it wasn't Lily.

> Bryan: This bachelorette party is bullshit.

> Kaiden: Feeling a little jealous, Hughes?

I smiled to myself. Everyone knew bachelorette parties could get pretty wild, but it was no different to a bachelor party. And besides, he had nothing to worry about where Carrie-Anne was concerned. They were solid.

> Bryan: So you're telling me you have zero problem with Lily going out dressed as a sexy cowgirl.

The fuck?

> Kaiden: Lily didn't say anything about that... she said they were going drinking and dancing, nothing crazy.

> Bryan: I don't think they all know. It's a surprise. They hired a VIP booth at some club in Harrisburg.

> Kaiden: But the moms are going, right?

> Bryan: The moms are the worst!!!

> Kaiden: They're grown women, Bry. They know how to make good choices.

Bryan: It's not their choices I'm worried about. Carrie-Anne showed me her outfit. Itty-bitty booty shorts and this crop top thing that barely covers her tits. They're going to draw all kinds of unwanted attention.

> Kaiden: I heard the guys are planning a stripper…

Bryan: That's different.

> Kaiden: I'm going to pretend you didn't say that. It's just a bachelorette party. What's the worst that can happen?

But the second I typed the words, doubt snaked through me, settling in the pit of my stomach. I trusted Lily—I trusted her implicitly. But I didn't trust other guys. Especially drunk guys around girls dressed as sexy cowgirls.

Double fuck.

Bryan: I'm just worried, Thatch. Sometimes I wonder what Caz even sees in me. She's so fucking smart and beautiful and I'm… me.

> Kaiden: I don't have time to be your therapist, man. I've got to be back out of the field in less than ten minutes.

> Bryan: How's it going?

> Kaiden: It's intense. But it feels right, ya know?

> Bryan: Always knew you'd go all the way. I'll let you get back to it. Be good to see you at the wedding.

I texted him a quick bye and wolfed down the rest of my lunch. Then I pulled up my message thread with Lily and sent her a quick message.

> Kaiden: Missing you. ILY xo

Before I could wait for her reply, Forest bellowed across the room, "Yo, Thatcher, let's go. I want to run those plays again."

"Coming." I switched off my cell, shoved it in my pocket, and headed toward my destiny.

LILY

"I'm not wearing that," I said, gawking at the baby pink cowboy hat Poppy held.

"You have to, it's the theme."

"The theme... you mean the theme no one told me about."

"Sweetheart," Mom said. "It was a surprise for Miley. You know how Cameron always jokes that Miley wrangled Avery—"

"Uncle Cam has never said that."

"I'm sure he said it at least once. Anyhow, we thought about what goes with *wrangled*... Cowboys... Sexy cowgirls."

"You've lost your mind," I murmured, hardly able to keep a straight face at the sight of her and Aunt Hailee in their matching hats and cowboy boots.

"We've still got it though, right?" Aunt Hailee grinned.

"Seriously, we've gotta wear the hats?"

"And the sashes!" Mom thrust a satin sash at me with the words 'last hoe down.'

"No, no way am I wearing—"

"Lily, you're here." Miley ran toward me and threw her arms around me. "Just go with it," she whispered in my ear.

"Hey, Miley. You look... nice."

"Isn't it fun?" She did a little twirl. "I didn't think we were doing a theme, but I love it. Don't you love it."

"Okay, what did you do to the bachelorette?" I asked no one in particular.

"Poppy opened a bottle of cherry sours." Miley winked at me, letting me know she'd been pretending to drink them.

"I bet she did." I rolled my eyes. "No more alcohol for you until we get to the club."

The club I didn't want to go to. But I'd promised to try and be a good sport for Miley's special night.

I was already late because I'd wanted to stop by and see Peyton. She had been officially discharged from the hospital but was finding it hard not to be with River twenty-four seven.

"Okay, you all need one of these." Poppy appeared with a tray of shot glasses. "We need to toast the bride-to-be before the car arrives."

An excited chorus of cheers went up around me as Ashleigh, Mrs. Fuller, Tara, Mya, and Carrie-Anne joined us.

"Gosh, this is exciting," Mrs. Fuller said, eagerly taking her shot.

"Miley," Poppy led us all in a toast. "Tonight is a chance to celebrate your last few days of freedom. Dance like no one's watching. Drink like you won't get sick. And party 'til we drop. Happy last hoe down. Cheers."

"Cheers." Everyone threw back their shots, but I

hesitated. This wasn't my idea of a good night but what the hell. Maybe a night of liquor-fueled fun was exactly what I needed.

"Lily, you've got to—"

I brought the glass to my lips and chucked it back, ignoring the slight burn.

"Atta girl," Mom applauded me, and I rolled my eyes.

"Okay, ladies." Mya checked her cell. "Our mighty steed awaits."

"Oh Jesus," I murmured under my breath right as Ashleigh came over.

"Just go with it. I find it's easier that way." She chuckled.

I'd thought things were bad with the cowboy hats and hoe down sashes but when we all filed out of Aunt Hailee's house, the pink Hummer limo was the definite icing on the cake.

"Oh. My. God." Miley shrieked with excitement. "You did this." She glanced at my mom, aunt, and Mya.

"We need to arrive in style."

"Hell, yes." Miley grabbed Tara's hand and pulled her toward the door.

"Ladies," the chauffeur said, doffing his cap.

"This is too much," Mrs. Fuller said.

"Not at all. Miley deserves this. Check out

inside. We added a few extras."

"Champagne?" Poppy's eyes lit up.

"On ice."

"Come on," Ashleigh said to me, and I followed them all to the Hummer.

"Ooh, there's snacks too." Poppy grabbed the chocolate covered strawberries. "Probably a good idea to line our stomachs."

The door closed behind me, and I sat on the plush leather bench running down one side of the luxurious Hummer.

"This is something else," Miley said, eyes slightly glazed from Poppy's encouragement.

"Selfie," Poppy hopped to the end of the vehicle with her back to us and held her phone up. "Say, last hoe down."

We all cheered the words, our laughter filling the limo. Even I managed to smile. It was gaudy and loud and completely over the top, but it was Miley's bachelorette. She deserved to feel special for the night.

"Okay, who wants champagne?" Mya asked, already pouring everyone a glass.

"Me, me, me, gimme." Poppy looked so happy. She liked a good party. "Sofe?"

"Hmm, maybe one or two. But I don't want a hangover tomorrow."

"It'll be worth it." Poppy winked at her. "Cole will take care of you, I'm sure."

"Pops," Sofia blushed, discreetly motioning to the moms.

"Oh girls, we were young once, you know," Mom said.

"Please God, no sex stories," I murmured.

"What? It's just a normal part of life, sweetheart. There's no need to be embarrassed. We all do it."

"Some more than others," Ashleigh muttered under her breath, aiming a knowing glance in Poppy's direction.

Poppy poked her tongue out and everyone laughed.

But I didn't laugh. Instead, I discreetly checked my cell phone to see if Kaiden had texted me. We'd talked earlier briefly until his teammates demanded his attention. Again.

It was impossible to have a proper conversation with him, and every day that passed only seemed to widen the distance between us.

So I was half-surprised to see a text message from him.

> Kaiden: How is the bachelorette party? Get into any trouble yet?

> Lily: I'm currently sitting in a pink Hummer limo drinking champagne in my pink cowboy hat and 'last hoe down' sash.

> Kaiden: You're kidding… I need to see that.

I snapped a quick selfie and forwarded it to him.

> Kaiden: Cute! I love the hat.

> Lily: I feel like a fool. As soon as we get to the club, I'm losing mine.

> Kaiden: You look beautiful, Lil. I wish I was there for a private dance, cowgirl.

I sucked in a sharp breath, the ache in my chest making itself known.

> Lily: God, I miss you.

> Kaiden: I know, babe. I know. But I'll see you next weekend hopefully.

> Lily: You'll make it, right?

> Kaiden: I cleared it with Coach so I'm 99% sure I'll make it.

> Lily: Good. Because I don't want to
> have to walk down the aisle with
> anyone but you.

> Kaiden: I'll be there.

My lips curved. The wedding was a week away. I could do that. I could survive another seven days without him.

> Lily: I'm going to hold you that xo

> Kaiden: Have fun, Lil. But not too
> much fun. ILY.

"Hey, no boyfriends," Poppy said, leaning over to snatch my phone out of my hand.

"You literally just texted Aaron a selfie."

"That was for him to distribute to the guys. Besides, I don't want you getting all mopey again. Tonight is a celebration. No sad faces allowed."

I forced a smile. Hoping she would buy it.

Hoping I would too.

CHAPTER FIFTEEN

KAIDEN

> Kaiden: Have you heard from the girls?

I hit send, hoping someone in the group chat would have an update.

> Aaron: Poppy is white girl wasted. I've had numerous video calls of her deep throating her straw.

> Bryan: Too much fucking information Bennet!

I snorted.

> Kaiden: Any updates on Lily? She stopped replying to me a while ago.

Ezra: Because your girl is probably grinding on some preppy douchebag.

> Kaiden: Fuck you, man. Fuck. You.

Gav: Relax, Thatchman, Lily is a good girl. If anyone's grinding on some preppy asshole, it's Poppy—sorry, Bennet. But your girl is a total party girl.

Aaron: And I wouldn't have her any other way. I'll never clip my girl's wings.

Cole: Even if she's getting hot and heavy on the dance floor with some other guy?

Aaron: Nothing you say will get under my skin. Poppy knows she'll never have it as good as she has it with me.

Ezra: Jesus, you're so full of bullshit.

I tried to get the conversation back on track.

> Kaiden: So no one knows if Lily's okay?

> Bryan: Want me to ask Caz for a Lily-update?

Did I?

Part of me did. I wanted to know if she was okay, that the girls were looking out for her.

But part of me didn't want to know what the hell they were up to on their 'last hoe down.'

Fuck.

> Ezra: Already handled. Ashleigh said Lily is fine. You don't need to worry. Leigh will look out for her.

> Aaron: You're so fucking boring. You could have told him that she's half-naked riding the mechanical bull or something.

Asshole. Before I could reply. Another message came through.

> Gav: Unless you want to ruin Thatcher's career before it's even started, I suggest you don't give him any ammunition to do something stupid like drive back to Rixon and hunt down his girlfriend.

> Kaiden: What he said!

> Aaron: I'm joking. We all know the two of you are endgame.

> Bryan: Maybe you should pop the question next week at the wedding.

> Cole: Dude. Wedding 101, no proposals.

> Bryan: I don't mean at the actual wedding, asshole. Like after, at the reception. That's romantic, right?

> Kaiden: I am not discussing this with you. I'll catch you later. Have fun at the bachelor party tomorrow.

> Aaron: Don't worry, I'll have enough fun for both of us.

I didn't doubt it. But I was still bummed about missing it. Football—joining an NFL team—meant sacrifice though, especially during the rookie phase.

I had to prove to everyone at the franchise that I wanted it. That I was willing to do whatever it took to ensure my name was on that roster.

Pay the price now, reap the rewards later.

At least, that's what I kept telling myself.

Still, there was something to be said about leaving your friends and family behind. Especially, your girlfriend—the love of your life. And knowing they were all spending one last summer together before everyone went their separate ways.

I opened up my message thread with Lily.

> Kaiden: I hope you're having fun. I miss you.

But she didn't reply.

Something was vibrating. I cracked an eye open to find the source of the irritation.

"Fucking answer that," my roommate grumbled.

Snatching my cell phone off the nightstand, I spied Lily's name, and a bolt of panic went through me.

It was late. Past two. Had something happened? Had—

"Hi my Mr. Football Player," she murmured down the line.

"Lily, what's going on?" I climbed out of bed and slipped into our en suite bathroom, locking the door.

"Poppy let me have my cell back, so I snuck off to the restrooms to call you."

"Restrooms?"

"Yeah, in the club."

"The club." Fuck. "You're still in the club?"

"Yeah. It's not as bad as I thought it would be. They gave us a VIP table with all these bottles of liquor and—"

"Jesus, Lil." I squeezed my eyes shut, rubbing my temples. "You're killing me here."

"Now you know how I feel." She hiccoughed. "Oops. I don't feel so good, Kaiden. I'm— Whoa."

"Lil? Lily?"

"The room is spinning. God, I wish you were here. I wish you were here and that I was there and that we were together. I hate this... I hate it so much."

The sheer desperation in her words split my chest in two, my heart damn near bleeding out.

"I know, babe. I know. It isn't easy for me either."

"But you have football. You *love* football."

"I love you, Lily May Ford."

"I know," she whispered but it got swallowed by a hiccough. "I just don't want you to love football more because I love you the way you love football."

"Lily, babe, what are you talking about?"

"Oh, I don't know." She let out a dramatic sigh. "Poppy and Carrie-Anne had me do all these shots and now everything is spinning and I'm here and you're there and I just really, really need you, Kaiden. I need you."

If her goal was torturing me, Lily had succeeded.

I fucking hated this. I hated knowing that she was there, and I was here, and her head was swimming with all these doubts and insecurities.

"Lily, listen to me."

"Mm-hmm."

"I love you. I love you so much and I can't wait for you to get here and for us to start our life together. It's you and me, babe. You and me."

"I loves you too." She let out a soft sigh. "You're my home, Kaiden. Without you, I'd be lost."

"Lily, babe, stop talking like this. We're fine." My voice cracked. "We're going to be fine."

I wanted to go to her. To get in my car and drive a thousand miles to Harrisburg and find her.

But I couldn't.

And for the first time since arriving in Kansas, I really fucking hated it.

"Babe, go find the girls. I'm going to text Ashleigh and Poppy."

"No... no, no, no. They'll be angry I called you. I wasn't supposed to call."

The fuck?

"What do you mean you weren't supposed to call me?"

"They didn't want me to get all sad and mopey. But they don't get it. Their boyfriends don't love football more than them."

"Lily..." I swallowed over the huge fucking lump in my throat. "I don't... that's not..."

But what could I say?

Lily was drunk and everyone's demons roared the loudest when they were inebriated.

"Go find the girls, babe. Now. I'm going to stay on the line until you find them, okay?"

"O-okay."

I put the call on speakerphone so I could pull up a new group chat with Ashleigh and Poppy.

> Kaiden: Can someone find Lily please. She's really drunk, and I'm worried about her.

> Ashleigh: Shit, she was right here. I'll go find her.

> Kaiden: Thank you. She's heading out of the restrooms.

"Lil?"

"Yeah?" I could hear the heavy din of the music in the background as she moved out into the club.

"Ashleigh is coming, so stay there—"

The line went dead, and panic fisted my heart.

> Poppy: Mr. Football! You shouldn't be calling Lilster. Tonight is a boyfriend-free zone.

> Kaiden: It's almost two and you know Lily doesn't handle getting drunk very well. And I think her cell just died.

> Poppy: Fuck. Is she okay? I thought she was having fun. We were helping her relax.

I rolled my eyes. Poppy meant well, and I knew she loved Lily something fierce. But they were like chalk and cheese.

> Kaiden: Just find her and get her home in one piece please.

> Poppy: Kaiden, come on. You know I'd never let anything happen to her. But it's not easy on her with you being there... starting your big new life without her.

> Ashleigh: Poppy, that isn't fair.

I stared at her words, trying to ignore the stab of pain I felt.

Is that what everyone thought?

Is that what Lily thought?

It wasn't like that.

I wanted her here. Fuck, I wanted her here more than anything, but I didn't want her to be here all alone while I was at camp.

> Poppy: Shit, Kaiden. I'm sorry, I shouldn't have said that. I'm drunk and I'm freaking out about Lil. We'll find her and make sure she's okay. I promise.

Locking down the guilt swimming in my stomach, I texted them back.

> Kaiden: I know. Just let me know she's okay, please.

Ten minutes.

Ten fucking minutes it took them to text me back and let me know Lily was okay and with them.

I managed to refrain from taking out my frustration on the hotel bathroom, slipping back into the room and getting into bed.

I needed to see her. To hold and kiss her.

I needed to look her in the eye and tell her that I was hers and she was mine, and that football would always be important to me but nothing, nothing was more important than her.

I couldn't do any of those things though.

All I could do was hope that once Lily saw me at the wedding, she would realize all her doubts were unfounded.

POPPY

"Oh my God," I groaned.

Everything hurt.

My muscles. My eyes. My stomach.

Definitely my stomach.

"Make it stop," someone else murmured.

"Ashleigh, is that you?" I lifted my hand up, trying to reach behind me.

"It's me." Fingers grazed mine.

"Lil?"

"Yeah."

"Where's Leigh?"

"In my room, I think. Why did I let you talk me into more shots?"

"Because it was fun," I said. "Because it seemed like the best idea at the time."

"I'm regretting it."

"Me too, Sis. Me too."

Gingerly, I rolled over to face Lily. She looked as rough as I felt. "You look like crap."

"I feel like it."

"How are you feeling, really?"

Her eyes glazed a little. "I'm okay. I'll be okay, Pops."

"Kaiden was really worried. I think I made him mad."

"Impossible." She forced a smile. "He knows you mean well."

"You've just been so sad since he left. I thought it would do you good to let loose a bit."

"I can't believe I drunk-dialed him." She threw her hand over her face, but I gently pried them away.

"Babe, he's your boyfriend. He loves you. Drunk-dialing is allowed."

"That's not what you said last night." She arched a brow.

"I was drunk, what did I know?" My lips twitched but she didn't take the bait.

"I hope I didn't say anything stupid."

"Kaiden wouldn't care. All he cared about was that you were okay."

"Yeah, I guess."

"Do you think Miley enjoyed herself?" I asked. "She seemed way too sober for a bachelorette party."

"I think Miley had the best time. We don't all need a ton of alcohol to have fun." Lily snickered but then her expression fell. "Pops, can I ask you something?"

"Anything, you know that."

"Do you think you and Aaron will get married?"

"One day, I hope. Sure. But I don't feel like I need a ring or anything to know that he loves me." I shrugged. "We're in a good place. I can wait until after college. Why do you ask?"

"Why do you think Kaiden hasn't asked me yet?"

My heart sank for her. Kaiden leaving had really fucked with her head. More than any of us realized. And the worst of it was, I didn't have an answer for her. Not one that would make it better anyway. So I said, "He's obviously waiting for the perfect moment."

"It's been almost five years," she said quietly.

"Don't do this, Lil. Don't overanalyze every little moment. You and Kaiden are one of the strongest, most together couples I know. You'll get through this. I know you will."

"I want to, I do. But I'm scared, Poppy. I'm so scared moving to Kansas will be the beginning of the end."

"Oh, babe. Come here." I pulled her into my arms and held her tight.

My sister wasn't like me. She didn't have thick skin and a strong sense of self-confidence. Even though college had hardened her to some degree she was still Lily.

"Everything is going to work out, you'll see," I said.

She peeked up at me and the uncertainty in her eyes made my heart ache. "And if it doesn't?"

"It will. Because Kaiden loves you, babe. He loves you."

"I know he does. That's not the issue."

"So what is then?"

A tear slipped free and rolled down her cheek. "What if it isn't enough?"

CHAPTER SIXTEEN

EZRA

"BUTTERCUP." I hovered over Ashleigh, stroking a finger down her cheek.

She swatted my hand away, murmuring, "Go away, I'm sleepy."

"You've been sleeping all day, it's time to wake up."

"Don't wanna." She grabbed the pillow and crushed it to her chest.

"Someone can't handle their liquor."

"Blame Poppy. She made me do shots."

I chuckled at her dramatics. "Don't be blaming Poppy for your own mistakes."

"I feel wrong."

"I have to get ready to leave soon but I could run you a bath?"

"No, no bath." She cracked an eye open, last night's makeup still smeared along her lashes.

"You want some Advil? Water? Coffee?"

"I know something that might make me feel better."

"Oh yeah?" I smirked.

"Lie with me?"

"Ten minutes."

Ashleigh pouted as I stripped out of my gray sweats and t-shirt and climbed into bed beside her.

I'd picked her up from the Fords' this morning, brought her home, and carried her straight up to my old room. Whatever they'd been drinking last night had wiped my girl out.

My lips curved. She was a cute drunk. I was disappointed I missed it.

"Come here." I half-pulled her onto my chest, sliding my hand into the back of her hair. "Love you, buttercup."

"Do you have to go?"

"You know I do. You got your fun last night. It's my turn."

"No strip clubs, right?"

"I don't want to lie to you..."

"Seriously." She poked her head up. "You think you'll end up in a strip club?"

"It's a bachelor party. Worst things could happen."

"Ugh," she grumbled. "I'm not a fighter but if any woman so much as tries to touch you…"

"Mmm," I nuzzled her neck. "I like it when you're all feisty and jealous."

"I just like you." She looped her arm around my neck and snuggled closer, hovering her mouth near mine.

"I'm not kissing you," I said, chuckling.

"What? Why?"

"Because you smell like you sank your body weight in cherry sours and tequila."

"I did. Poppy made me do it."

"Poor baby."

"You could kiss me and make it all better."

"Not going to happen, buttercup." I pecked the end of her nose. "Because if I kiss you, I'll end up inside you, and I need to get ready."

"Ugh, E. You can't say things like that to me."

Laughter filled the room as I kissed her forehead and climbed out of bed. "You should think about getting up and getting something to eat and drink. Asher made Mom pancakes, they helped."

"I'm going to stay right here until you get back."

"It'll be late."

"Then you'd better find a way to wake me up."

"Tease!"

She smiled, gazing up at me with so much love I felt ten fucking feet tall.

"If you're going to stay here until I'm home, can you at least do me a favor?" I said.

"Sure, anything."

"Take a shower, buttercup. You stink."

ASHLEIGH

"Leigh, sweetheart, do you need anything?" Mya called from beyond Ezra's door.

"No thanks, I'm good."

"Okay, well you know where I am if you need me."

I loved staying over at the Bennets'. It never felt weird or uncomfortable. Mya and Asher treated me like one of their own and I loved them for it.

How could I not when they'd taken in the boy I loved more than anything in the world?

I rolled onto my side and reached over for my cell phone, checking for an update from Ezra. Apparently Aaron had incited a stupid no girlfriends rule too. He and Poppy were as bad as each other.

Despite how awful I felt today, last night had

been fun. Spending the night with my best friends, my mom, and the women in our expanding family. Miley had loved every second, and she deserved it.

I couldn't wait to see her walk down the aisle next weekend and watch her and my brother tie the knot.

Our first wedding.

It was exciting.

I suspected it would also be the catalyst for a few more engagements and wedding bells.

Opening up the group chat, I texted the girls.

> Ashleigh: Any updates?

> Poppy: Aaron sent me a sneaky video of Avery attempting to play golf blindfolded. They sure know how to have fun...

I laughed, typing out my reply.

> Ashleigh: Scandalous. Although, I'm sure they're saving the real fun for tonight.

> Poppy: Ugh. Don't remind me.

> Ashleigh: How are you feeling, Lily?

She didn't reply.

Sofia: I'm fine, thanks for asking.

> Ashleigh: We know you're fine, Sofe. You drank like three drinks and switched to water.

Sofia: Because I'm smart.

Poppy: Have you talked to Miley, Leigh? How is she feeling?

> Ashleigh: Her and Tara are off enjoying afternoon tea with her mom.

Poppy: How? How? My stomach is still churning…

> Ashleigh: Well, you did insist on that last round of shots.

Poppy: I'm an idiot.

Lily: I love you, Pops.

Sofia: Hey, Lil. You good?

Lily: I'm okay.

> Ashleigh: Any word from Kaiden?

Lily: We spoke briefly earlier.

Sofia: I bet he can't wait until next weekend.

Lily: Yeah.

Ashleigh: The wedding is going to be so much fun.

Poppy: Does anyone want to go for pizza later? I might be ready to try and eat something by then.

Ashleigh: I'm embracing a day in my pjs.

Sofia: I could eat pizza.

Poppy: Text me later then. Lil?

Ashleigh: You do know you could go and ask her right? She's in the bedroom down the hall.

Poppy: I can't move right now for fear of puking.

Ashleigh: I'm going to watch mindless TV until Ezra gets home.

Poppy: Good luck with that. If he's anything like Aaron, he'll come in, fall over trying to get out of his clothes and puke all over himself.

> Ashleigh: Nah, not my E. He's more sensible than that.

> Poppy: We'll see. Bachelor parties are something else, Leigh xo

---

My eyes fluttered open at the sound of a baby elephant entering the room. "Ezra?" I murmured.

"Shh, buttercup. Go back to sleeping."

Pushing up on one elbow, my eyes strained against the darkness to find him stumbling around, trying to take his pants off. "Why Ezra Bennet, are you drunk?" I chuckled.

"Shh." He pressed a finger to his lips. "Don't wake Mya. Ash doesn't want her to know he's wasted."

"Pretty sure Mya knows exactly what Ash is like after a few drinks."

"I missed you." He started toward the bed, legs still in his pants.

"Ezra, wait—"

He went down like a sack of bricks, his body landing with a resounding *thud*.

"Fuck," he groaned.

"Jesus, E." I slipped out of bed and went to him. "You okay down there?"

"I'm fucked, buttercup. I'm so fucking fucked."

With an amused grin, I went back to the bed and grabbed the pillows and coverlet and joined Ezra on the floor.

"What are you doing?" he asked as I tucked a pillow underneath his head.

"We can sleep down here."

"No. No, no, no... I want to fuck you in my bed."

"Babe, I don't think you can see straight let alone fuck me right now."

God, he was cute like this. All carefree and playful.

Ezra didn't let his walls down often. Even now, even after years of loving him, he was careful with his heart and humor and trust.

So to be on the inside, to be privileged enough to see him like this, was a gift I would never take for granted.

"I reckon I can get it up." He gave me a lazy grin. "You might have to coax him a little though."

I managed to get his pants off but didn't bother trying to remove his polo shirt. Then I pulled the cover over us and curled into his side. "Did you have fun?" I asked.

"Yeah. I thought I'd hate it... but I didn't."

"And Avery? Did he have a good time?"

"He's a fucking mess. Ash and Jase got him and your dad into all kinds of trouble."

"Why am I not surprised. But everyone made it home in one piece?"

"They did." Ezra hooked his arm around my neck and pulled me closer, the bitter scent of liquor wafting over my face.

I didn't care though.

I didn't care one bit.

"You want that one day, buttercup?"

"What?" I played dumb.

"The crazy bachelorette party and big white wedding."

"You know none of that is important to me. I'd be happy with a small wedding by the lake with our families."

"One day, Leigh Leigh." He kissed my brow. "One day."

I liked the sound of that.

But I was in no rush, content with living. Loving. Having adventures together.

"It was a shame Kaiden couldn't make it," he murmured, his fingers stroking along my waist.

"Yeah. But at least he'll be here for the wedding.

"Mm-hmm."

"Love you, E."

"Love you, buttercup."

Ezra was asleep in seconds, his gentle snores filling the room.

But I didn't sleep. Not yet.

I laid there, cuddled up to the boy I loved.

The boy I'd watched turn into one of the best men I knew.

Ezra hadn't had the best start in life. Until the Bennets took him in, he didn't know what it was like to be loved or respected or cherished. But I'd spend the rest of my life showing him.

Because I was his anchor.

And he was my home.

"Shit, I think I'm dying."

The familiar gravel of Ezra's voice pulled me from a deep sleep.

"Good morning." I smiled at him.

"There is nothing good about how I feel right now."

"Now you know how I felt yesterday. Can you remember getting in?" I asked.

"I can vaguely remember you taking my pants off. The rest is hazy."

"Sign of a good night. Dare I ask if there were strippers involved?"

"We didn't go to a strip club, much to Mr. Fuller's disappointment." Ezra's brow furrowed, the sunlight glinting off his piercing. "But the guys, Jase and Ash had arranged a little surprise for Avery."

"Oh my God. I would have paid to see that."

"She was very... aggressive."

"Jesus." I barely contained my laughter. "And what about you, stud?" My fingers glided down his washboard abs. "Did you have a private dance?"

"Not my thing." He grabbed my ass and pulled me closer. "Besides, why would I want to look at another woman when I get to come home every night to you."

"Right answer."

"You think you can eat? We could go out—"

"I think I need breakfast in bed."

"Oh, you do, huh?"

"Naked breakfast in bed." He grinned.

"Well, you're not getting anywhere near me until you've showered, mister."

"I'll shower, you make breakfast and meet back here in thirty?"

"Deal."

I got up and waited for him to follow. But the

second he got upright, it was apparent a shower might be a little difficult.

"Holy shit, I think I'm still drunk."

"You need a little help there?" I chuckled, watching with amusement as he tried to steady himself.

"Change of plans." He smirked, his eyes hooded with desire. "Breakfast can wait, I think I need you to help me shower first."

CHAPTER SEVENTEEN

LILY

"HOW IS SHE?" I whispered as I slipped into the hospital room.

"She's okay. Enjoying cuddles with her mama." Peyton beamed, some of the shadows in her eyes gone from the last time I saw her.

"Oh, Peyton, she's beautiful."

"She's so small. I keep thinking I'm going to hurt her." She gazed down at her daughter with so much love it made my heart cinch.

"Can I?" I motioned to the chair next to them and Peyton nodded.

"River has been looking forward to seeing her Aunt Lily again."

"Hi, sweet girl." I gently held her finger in mine,

careful not to get tangled up in the wires.

Every day, River was getting stronger. And every day was another day closer to her being able to go home with Xander and Peyton. But it would be a little while yet.

"How was the bachelorette party? Tell me everything."

"I'd rather not," I mumbled.

"Why? What happened?"

"I got drunk."

"Scandalous." She chuckled.

"No, I mean, I got really drunk, Peyton. And I drunk-dialed Kaiden."

"Oh, well that's not too bad."

"It's not good! What if I said something horrible?"

"Come on, Lil. This is you. You don't have a mean bone in your body."

"True. But I've been feeling off-kilter since he left."

"Well, have you spoken to him since then?" I nodded, and she said, "And? What did he say?"

"He didn't say anything really. Just wanted to know if I was okay."

"Then don't sweat it. Men are simple creatures. If you'd have said anything to upset him, I'm sure he would have said so."

River started fussing in her arms, and she gently rocked her.

"You're a natural," I said.

"I don't feel like one. Everything is so new and scary. I'm a mess."

"You're a mom." My lips curved. "How's Xander handling everything?"

"Honestly, he's been my rock. I don't know what I would have done without him. He's about the only thing keeping me sane."

"Hopefully it'll be a little bit easier now she's allowed out more."

"I hope so. I just want to bring her home. I'm missing out on so much." Emotion filled her voice.

"I know it feels like that but she's here to get strong. You'll still get to have all those firsts."

She pressed her lips into a thin line, doubt shining in her eyes. I couldn't claim to know what it was like to watch your child hooked up to all kinds of machines, so tiny and fragile. But I could see Peyton's love for River. The utter adoration in her gaze as she watched over her daughter.

"We're not going to come to the wedding," she said. "I already told Avery and Miley."

"We didn't think you would."

"I just... I can't be there, pretending to enjoy myself when she's here, all alone."

"Everyone understands. But we'll miss you. All of you."

"You'll have to see if you can sneakily video them saying their vows."

"I'll see what I can do." I chuckled softly.

"Kaiden's coming home for the wedding?"

"Yeah. They have that weekend free."

"I bet you can't wait to see him."

"I'm both excited and nervous... Silly, right?"

"I don't think so. Things haven't been easy on either of you the last few weeks."

"I just didn't know I'd find it so hard. I know it sounds ridiculous and super co-dependent, but I'd gotten used to having him around. Knowing that if things got too hard, he'd be there to make everything better."

"He's your person, Lil. There's nothing wrong with that. But you've come so far, babe. You're stronger than you think, you know."

"I just keep thinking what if I get to Kansas and I hate it."

"Lily, look at me." I lifted my gaze to Peyton, and she offered me a small, understanding smile. "You can't keep doing this. Kaiden loves you. And you love him. You have to trust that everything will work out the way it's supposed to."

"But what if it doesn't?" My stomach churned

violently, a feeling that had been growing bigger and bigger ever since Kaiden had left.

It was silly, part of me knew that. But I also couldn't keep the doubt at bay. I couldn't stop myself from getting swept up in the panic.

"You need to reframe that thought to what if it does." Her smile grew. "I have spent four years watching you come out of your shell, Lil. Four years of loving and laughing and living. Football doesn't change that. Moving to Kansas doesn't change that. You and Kaiden are meant to be, babe. That's all you need to trust in."

She made it sound so simple. But my mind was a messy place to be.

"You're not hair pulling again, right?"

"No." I shook my head. "I haven't for a long time."

Sometimes the urge came over me, especially in times of heightened stress or anxiety. But I controlled it now, it didn't control me.

"I think you need to talk to Kaiden after the wedding. Get all these thoughts off your mind. You should be looking forward to the next chapter of your life together."

"I know… you're right."

"But it doesn't make it any easier to believe."

I nodded again.

"You've got this, Lil. Everything is going to be fine. Now, how would you like to hold your niece?"

"For real? I didn't think—"

"It's okay. She's ready to meet you properly, aren't you, beautiful girl." Peyton carefully got up and brought River over to me. "You need to cradle her head but don't put too much pressure on her. She's only tiny."

"Okay." I gulped, suddenly feeling very out of my depth. "Wait, maybe I shouldn't—"

"It's fine. You won't break her." Peyton laid River in my arms, and I swear I stopped breathing.

She felt so tiny and fragile, I was scared to move.

"There you go. See, easy."

I gawked at Peyton as she moved back to sit in her chair. "She's so tiny."

"Tiny but strong."

"She's perfect."

She really was.

Emotion swelled inside me, a deep sense of protectiveness and love. It was natural, she was my best friend's baby, after all.

But it was something else too.

I wanted this. I wanted a family. And Peyton was right, when I looked into the future, I only saw one man by my side, sharing my life with me.

Kaiden.

KAIDEN

I couldn't get Lily's words from the night of the bachelorette party out of my head.

All week, I'd replayed them over and over, trying to figure out what was the liquor talking and what was her.

I'd always known she would find it hard when the time came for me to leave for camp, but I'd clearly underestimated the impact it would have.

Surely, she didn't genuinely believe that I loved football more than I loved her.

Football was my passion, my dream. But she was my home. My heart. Without Lily, I wouldn't be the man I was today, the football player I was.

So it had fucking gutted me to hear her so defeated and upset the other night.

I hadn't asked her about it though. I didn't want to embarrass her any more than I knew she already felt.

But not talking about it was killing me.

"Jesus Christ, Thatcher," the offensive coordinator yelled as I fumbled another pass. "Get your head in the game."

I gave him a tense nod.

He was right to cuss me out, I was off my game. I'd managed to cover it up yesterday and the day before that. But the cracks were starting to show. Because I couldn't get my mind off Lily.

It was full steam ahead for Saturday's wedding, so they were all busy. But being a bridesmaid, Lily seemed to shoulder a lot of the burden.

Another twenty minutes of running the plays and sweat rolled down my back. The heat was brutal, but I'd come out here and forced my discomfort into a little box.

That was half the battle with football. You had to compartmentalize. You had to shove all the background noise, all the distractions, away and focus one hundred and ten percent on the game.

I could do that with the heat or the slight ache in my left shoulder.

I couldn't do that with Lily.

She was woven into my DNA, the very fabric of my soul. I couldn't just put her in a box and forget about her.

But I also needed to get my head out of my ass and play a better game. I'd come too far to drop the ball now. Literally.

"Think you can manage to make the pass this time?" One of the rookies shouted with a smirk.

I let their taunt roll off my back as I found my player on the left side of the field, and called the play.

The center snapped the ball to me and I dropped

back, letting the defense barrel toward me. The running back swept in front of me, seemingly taking the ball and sprinting off down field. The second he commanded everyone's attention, I hiked up my arm and sent the ball flying toward the wide receiver.

It was a clean pass, and relief slammed into me as the receiver leapt high, hooking his hand around the ball and pulling it into his body as he took off toward the end zone.

"About fucking time," someone murmured.

I didn't look to see who it was.

It didn't matter.

I'd made the pass, I'd proved my worth.

"Okay," Coach yelled, his heavy gaze settled in my direction. "That's more like it, Thatcher. Now run it again."

"You wanna talk about it?" Forest asked.

"Nope." I shoved a piece of chicken into my mouth.

Three days.

Three days until I head back to Rixon and got to see Lily.

We talked here and there. But it was still

strained and more often than not, we were interrupted by the team or the girls. At this precise moment in time, our lives weren't our own and we were both just trying to keep our heads above water.

But over the weekend, I planned on reminding her as much as possible that she was my number one girl. And that while I loved football and wanted a career in the NFL so much, it didn't come close to how I felt about her.

"Let me guess... girl troubles?"

"I'm not doing this," I said, and his mouth quirked.

"What'd I tell you man, it's not worth it."

"She's worth it."

She was worth every goddamn thing.

"So you won't be sticking around on the weekend then?"

"Hell no. The second we get done with practice Friday, I'm out of here. Got the red-eye back to Philadelphia."

"Nice. I'm sticking around. Some of the guys are going exploring."

"You don't want to go home and see your family?"

"Nah."

He didn't say any more, and I didn't ask. A lot of

us were still guarded, not wanting to get too close in case we didn't make the cut.

But I hoped if I made it, Forest would be right there beside me. He was a good guy and an even better player.

My cell vibrated and I smiled.

"Your girl?"

I nodded, snatching it up and opening Lily's message.

> Lily: I didn't think it was possible, but Aunt Hailee has turned into bridezilla.

> Kaiden: Isn't that what you're supposed to call the bride?

> Lily: She might as well be for the way she's freaking out.

> Kaiden: Everything is going to be perfect. I can't wait to see you in your dress.

> Lily: It's not what I would have picked. But it's Miley's big day.

> Kaiden: Atta girl. I'm counting down until Saturday.

> Lily: Me too. What time does your flight get in?

> Kaiden: Early. Like four. I'll wake you up with a kiss.

> Lily: I've missed you so much, Kaiden.

> Kaiden: Soon, babe.

> Lily: How's practice going?

> Kaiden: I messed up a bit this morning. Got a girl on my mind.

> Lily: Kaiden, you have to focus.

My lips twitched. She cared. Lily still cared. She was just struggling, and I got it. Because I was too. But it wasn't forever. In fact...

> Kaiden: I got the name of a realtor from one of the guys. Maybe we can check out some places online over the weekend.

> Lily: Okay xo

Not quite the answer I was hoping for. But it was only three more days.

Three days until I got to hold my girl in my arms.

Three days until I got to show her how much I loved her.

CHAPTER EIGHTEEN

SOFIA

"COLE," I said. "You're staring again."

"Yeah, because you look so... Fuck, Sofe. You're killing me here."

Heat flooded my cheeks as I dipped my head to take a rather large sip of champagne.

He hadn't taken his eyes off me, and it was starting to make me feel uncomfortable.

Uncomfortable in the best possible way.

"Sofia Bennet"—he leaned in, letting his mouth brush the shell of my ear—"you wouldn't happen to be blushing, would you?"

"Cole!"

"Back up, son," Dad's hearty laughter filled the

room, and suddenly the entire rehearsal dinner party was looking in our direction.

"Dad," I hissed.

"What?" He gave me innocent puppy dog eyes, but his mouth quirked up. He knew exactly what he was doing.

"Ash," Mom chided. "Stop embarrassing her."

"The boy has barely taken his eyes off her. It's not appropriate for—"

"Ash!"

A grunt of pain spilled out of Dad, and I figured Mom had slammed her stiletto heel down on his foot or jabbed him in the ribs, maybe.

Either way, he shut up and we were able to eat the rest of the delicious three course meal in peace.

The rehearsal wedding had gone off without a hitch. I hadn't liked watching Lily walk down the aisle alone but at least Kaiden would be there tomorrow.

She was quiet. Even quieter than usual. I'd tried to talk to her about it, but the day had been a flurry of activity with the final touches being made here and there.

Hailee and Mrs. Fuller had done an incredible job though. The venue was perfect. The decorations were impeccable. And the little details were a celebration of Avery and Miley's love. Right down to the splashes of black and gold, paying homage to Avery's team the Steelers, or the gold-tipped lilies which signified Miley's favorite flower.

It was beautiful, and I couldn't help but imagine what I wanted my own wedding day to be like.

After the dessert plates were collected up, Cameron stood to give his speech. He looked so smart in his charcoal suit, his tie matching the shimmering gold of Hailee's dress.

Silence ushered over the room, and he started. "Hello, for those of you who don't know, I'm Cameron, the father of the groom. I'd like to start by thanking my wife Hailee and Miley's mom Christine for arranging this beautiful rehearsal dinner and making us all feel so welcome tonight.

"All any parent wants for their child is to be happy. To have purpose and to find love. And my wife and I could not be prouder to be standing here on the precipice of Miley and Avery's big day."

Tears filled my eyes and Cole reached for my hand under the table, squeezing tight.

There was something so beautiful about this moment. About the amount of love in the room.

We were no longer kids with big dreams and hopes for the future. We were adults now. With our own lives, making those childhood dreams come true.

"Avery," Cameron went on. "Watching the man

you have become has been a wonderful thing. We are so proud of you, Son. You love almost as well as you play football."

That earned him a laugh from every person in the room.

"But it's Miley who really deserves the credit here. Miley, sweetheart, it has been a joy getting to know you and watching you love our son the way we could only hope for.

"It isn't easy standing beside a professional athlete, but you do it with grace and humility and we are proud to welcome you into our family." He cleared his throat. "I don't want to bore you all half to death, but before we raise a glass to your wedding day, I do want to impart one piece of advice to Miley and Avery.

"Choose each other. Even when life gets tough, even when things don't perhaps go your way, choose each other. Choose your relationship. Choose your life together. Do that and you'll be okay.

"Now please join me in raising our glasses to Avery and Miley, and the love I hope they'll share for years to come!"

Their names rang out around me as we toasted the happy couple, and I looked around, hardly surprised there wasn't a dry eye in the room.

"One day," Cole whispered.

"One day." I grinned, my heart so full of joy and pride. We were lucky. To have these friends, this family.

And if life had taught me anything, it was to cherish the little moments.

KAIDEN

"Fuck," I checked the time on my phone. "I'm not going to make it."

"You'll make it," Forest said as he began stripping out of his sweat-soaked jersey.

Final practice before our weekend break had been a shitshow. The coaching staff decided to keep us here longer than expected, which meant I had less than two hours to get to the airport, and the airport was almost fifty minutes away.

"Yeah, if I don't shower and manage to get an Uber driver who will break every speed limit between here and the airport."

"Dude, you've got to take a shower. You're a fucking mess."

He wasn't wrong.

We were all covered in mud and grass stains thanks to the sudden downpour that had made practice a real messy affair.

"Go," he urged. "Be quick."

I pulled off my shoulder pads and unlaced my pants, pushing them down my hips.

Lily would be at the rehearsal dinner by now.

I fucking hated that she had to walk down the aisle by herself for the rehearsal, but I would be there tomorrow.

Anything else was not an option.

Grabbing my soap and towel, I headed for the showers and made quick work of washing the grime off me. Today had been tough, physically and mentally, and I was looking forward to a couple of days off with my friends and family to clear my head and regroup.

Two weeks without Lily had been nothing short of torture and I couldn't wait to spend two nights with her.

When I was done, I towel dried my hair before slinging it around my waist and heading back to my locker to get changed.

"Big plans for the weekend?" Chad asked.

"Going home to my girl."

"Nice. Flying out tomorrow?"

"No, I'm on the red-eye out of Topeka."

"You might want to check the travel alerts. I heard there's been a big accident on the highway."

"What?"

"Yeah." He nodded. "Sounds bad. The place is at a standstill."

"Fuck," I breathed, grabbing my phone and opening the local news app. Sure enough there was the alert.

"Is there another route to the airport?"

"You'd have to take the Kansas turnpike and come back around. It'll add like a good thirty, forty minutes onto your journey."

I didn't have forty minutes.

I needed to leave in the next fifteen minutes if I wanted to make check-in. Adding another thirty minutes onto that wasn't going to work.

"Maybe I can get a later flight," I said to no one in particular, my mind already running over every scenario.

I couldn't drive, it was over a thousand miles, and the Greyhound would take almost sixteen hours. Flying was the only option if I was going to get there in time for tomorrow.

I sat down and checked the flight schedule. "Fuck."

There was nothing. Nothing that didn't involve a connecting flight anyway.

And I didn't have time.

I had to be there tomorrow morning, or I would miss the wedding.

"There's a flight out of Kansas City at five to midnight. It goes via O'Hare," Forest said. "But it'll put you in Harrisburg International at six in the morning. That's enough time to make it to Rixon, right?"

"Yeah, that'll work."

I hadn't thought to look for flights out of other nearby airports.

"I could kiss you right now," I said.

"Please don't." He grimaced. "But you should probably get moving. You have a flight to catch."

"Kaiden?" Lily said the second she answered.

"Thank fuck," I breathed, "my battery is almost dead."

"What's the matter?"

"I just wanted to let you know that I didn't make my flight—"

"What? What do you mean you didn't make it?" Panic coated her voice. "The wedding is tomorrow."

"I know, I know. There was a huge pile up on the highway and I couldn't get there in time. But I managed to book a flight out of Kansas City. I'm here now."

"You have another flight?"

"Yeah. There's a connection in O'Hare so I won't get in until about six. But I should be in Rixon with time to spare."

"Thank God. I thought you were going to tell me you couldn't make it."

"I told you I'd be there, and I meant it. I need to see my girl."

"It's been the longest two weeks of my life," she said, failing to hide the sadness in her voice.

All I wanted was to hold her. To reassure her we were okay. That I loved her, and she loved me and that was enough.

"I know, babe. But we have the whole weekend. I don't have to be back in Kansas until Tuesday morning. Three whole days."

"I like the sound of that."

"I just wanted to let you know before my cell dies. I forgot to grab my charger, but I'll buy one once I'm through security."

"Okay," she said. "Thanks for calling."

"Of course. I love you."

"I love you too. See you tomorrow. Text me before takeoff."

"I will. Bye."

"Bye." She hung up and I let out a small sigh.

The strain was a permanent thing between us

now, but it was nothing a weekend together wouldn't erase.

I'd make sure of it.

I made it through check-in and security and found a quiet seat near the gate. A few people glanced my way, probably trying to figure out where they recognized me from. That was going to get a lot more regular come the fall, when I hopefully made my debut appearance for the Wild.

It was the part of the job I was least looking forward to. I just wanted to play football. I didn't need the rest of it—the fame and fortune and notoriety. I still wanted to be able to take Lily out and enjoy our life together.

I couldn't promise her that I would never get noticed but I could promise her that we would keep our lives as private as possible.

Because I was content with spending my time off with her. Lazy weekends in our apartment. Flying back to Rixon to see our friends and family. I wanted football, but I also wanted a quiet life.

A life full of love and laughter and my best friend. My partner in crime.

My girl.

I wanted a life with Lily.

A long happy life with the woman I loved.

CHAPTER NINETEEN

AARON

"PSST, POPPYSTAR." I tried to catch her attention, but my eyes had a life of their own, focusing on her ass in that second skin of a dress.

It was... fuck.

"Poppy," I whisper-hissed.

She finally glanced around, frowning when she spotted me. I beckoned her over and she hurried toward me. "What are you doing? You're not supposed to be back here."

"Sorry, but it couldn't wait. Fuck, you look beautiful." The pale gold dress really complemented her skin tone, accentuating her curves in a way that had my mind in very dirty places.

"You came back here to tell me I look beautiful?" Her frown deepened.

"Yes, I mean, no. No, that's not... this dress is very distracting."

"Focus, Aaron," she snapped. "The wedding starts in less than an hour. Lily is completely freaking out because Kaiden's not here yet and Miley can't stop crying. It's a disaster back here, I don't need you—"

"He isn't going to make it."

"What do you mean he isn't going to make it? Avery's here, I've seen him. I was right—"

"Not Avery, Kaiden."

"What?" she shrieked.

"Shh. I'm trying not to cause a fuss."

"A fuss? A fuss? Kaiden has to be here. He's walking down the aisle with Lily. It's been the only thing getting her through."

"He just called, his flight got diverted and he's stuck in Columbus."

"I can't believe this is happening. How the hell am I going to tell her he's not coming. She's going to be devastated."

"It's not his fault, he—"

"Not helping right now." She snapped. "God, this is the worst thing that could happen. He promised her."

"Shh." I pulled her into my arms, careful not to touch her hair which was in some fancy updo. "It'll be okay. Hopefully he'll be here later, and everything will be fine."

Poppy gazed up at me with a sad expression. "This will break her, Aaron. She's already riding the edge. Once she realizes he isn't coming…"

"Yeah, I know."

Lily had struggled the last couple of weeks. She put on a brave face and went about life with a smile, but we'd all seen the cracks.

Kaiden was her person. Her rock. Without him, her foundations were shaky.

"Do you want me to tell her?" I asked because I would. I'd do anything to make my girl's life easier.

"No." She let out a soft, resigned sigh. "It should be me. But you need to text Kaiden and tell him if he doesn't make it here, to not bother coming back at all because I swear to God, I'll kill him. I'll kill him, Aaron."

"Pop—"

"Don't Poppy me. One day. The one day she needed him, and he didn't make it."

She ripped out of my hold and marched back toward the bridal party. I watched from the door. Watched as she pulled Lily to one side and told her.

Watched as Lily's expression crumpled, and she started crying.

Fuck.

Kaiden had really messed up. But it wasn't his fault. His life wasn't his own right now. Throw in a bad traffic accident, a two hour delay at Kansas City, and a diverted aircraft and there wasn't much he could do.

I left the girls to it, and pulled out my cell as I headed back to the groom's party.

> Aaron: Hey, man. I just broke the news to Poppy. I know shit is out of your control but a word of advice... find a way to get here. Stat.

> Kaiden: I'm working on it.

> Kaiden: How'd she take it?

I knew he didn't mean Poppy.

> Aaron: Just get here as fast as you can.

LILY

Tears streaked down my face as I walked down the flower-lined aisle with my head held high.

Miley wanted to ask one of her cousins to stand

in for Kaiden, but I refused. I wanted no one else beside me except Kaiden. And he wasn't here.

He wasn't here.

The second Poppy had stood before me to deliver the news, I'd known.

Kaiden wasn't going to make it.

He broke his promise.

In that moment, it didn't matter that it wasn't his fault. It didn't matter that the odds had been stacked against him the second he left the Wild's facility just outside of Topeka.

The little voices in my head didn't care.

Kaiden wasn't coming, and all I could think was it was a perfect example of everything I'd been worried about.

Football was his priority now.

Not me.

Inhaling a shuddering breath, I kept walking. My hands clutched around the flower posy as if it was somehow holding me upright.

Tara and Flint walked ahead of me with Ashleigh and Ezra, Poppy and Cole, and Sofia and Aaron behind me. And although I didn't see people's confusion at my lack of a groomsman, I felt it. Like tiny shards of glass cutting into me. Over and over.

When I finally reached the front of the room and joined Tara, I released a small sigh of relief.

I'd made it and I hadn't completely fallen apart.

Mom caught my eye and gave me a reassuring smile, but it did nothing to ease the pain in my chest.

I knew some people wouldn't get it. They wouldn't understand why it mattered so much. I was a strong independent woman, I could understand and accept why my boyfriend had to prioritize football camp. It was his shot at greatness. Something few people ever got to achieve.

And part of me did get it. The rational, levelheaded part that knew Kaiden would be beating himself up over the fact he wasn't here. But I wasn't always rational or levelheaded.

Despite all my progress since high school, every day I fought with my mind, the negative thoughts and crippling anxiety. Every day, I fought hard to ignore the dark corners of my heart where my childhood pain and trauma lived.

Those parts of me didn't get it.

They didn't care if the flight got diverted. Or if the Wild's coaching staff made their team stay late to practice.

They just didn't care.

And if I gave them enough attention, I was almost sure I could hear them whisper, *we told you so.*

"Oh, Avery, I'm so happy for you." I hugged my cousin tightly. "It was such a beautiful ceremony."

He pulled back to look at me. "How are you holding up?"

"I'm fine." My smile felt tight, but it was hard work maintaining the illusion.

"It isn't his fault," he said, sympathy shining in his eyes.

"I know."

"Do you though? Because Kaiden is going to get here, he'll be here, Lily. And it'll be three days."

Two and a half now but who was counting?

"Don't waste them fighting when we all know how much you've missed him."

"Maybe it's a sign," I whispered, surprised I'd let the words tumble out.

My deepest fear.

"A sign... Shit. You think... No. No way. Not today, Lil. You hear me. Kaiden loves you. He loves you, cuz. And he's going to need you more than ever come the start of the season."

"I'm not sure I'm cut out for this life, Avery. I thought I could do it." Tears sprang into my eyes again, and I hated that I wasn't stronger. I hated myself so much for not being able to suppress my emotions on Avery's special day.

"I'm sorry, I'm a mess. You should go and find your bride. I'm sure she's looking for you."

"Just hang in there, yeah." He leaned in and kissed my cheek before taking off to find Miley.

"Oh, Lil." Poppy came up beside me and wrapped her arm around me, laying her head on my shoulder. "He'll be here."

"Yeah."

I hadn't checked my phone, I couldn't.

I didn't want to see his apologies—his excuses.

This was a day of celebration, not mourning. I didn't want to ruin everyone's day with my disappointment.

Not that I was doing a very good job of hiding it.

"Come on," she said. "We need to take our seats."

So I followed her to our table, staring at the empty seat beside my place card.

God, this was horrible. Everybody close to me understood, they got it. But it didn't stop my agony as I sat down, knowing that the seat beside me would remain empty until Kaiden got here.

If he got here.

Aaron had told Poppy that Kaiden was determined to make it but Columbus was over five hours away.

The food smelled amazing, but I barely tasted it. The speeches incited laughter and tears but I only heard white noise. And when the newlyweds walked onto the dance floor to have their first dance, I could hardly see them because of the tears in my eyes.

I was a mess.

And it was all Kaiden's fault.

"Lily," Poppy said we're supposed to join them for the end of the first dance.

"You go," I shrugged.

How the hell did she expect me to go out there without a partner?

"Sweetheart." Dad appeared. "Can your old man have this dance?" He held out his hand, but I hesitated. "Lily, let's go."

"Fine." I took his hand and let him lead me onto the dance floor. Poppy and Ashleigh both gave me a reassuring smile but I didn't return it.

I was too lost in my own thoughts. The little voices whispering all kinds of cruel things.

"Talk to me, Lil. I'm worried." Dad swayed us to the soft melody of Avery and Miley's first dance.

"I know I'm overreacting," I said, unable to look him in the eye. "But it's like senior year all over again when I saw him at Homecoming with Lindsey Filmer."

"Lily, sweetheart, you know this is not the

same. Kaiden can't control airplanes or the weather, he can't ditch rookie camp to fly home for a wedding that's not his own. It doesn't work like that."

"I know." I lifted my eyes to his. "I'm not handling things very well, Dad. And I wish I wasn't like this, I wish I could be different—"

"Whoa, Lily. None of us want you to be different. Least of all, Kaiden. But you need to take a breath and try to come at things from a rational place.

"You knew it was going to be hard. But it's one summer, sweetheart. One summer and then the rest of your lives." He pressed a chaste kiss to my forehead, and I soaked up his comfort.

"I love you, Dad," I said.

"I love you too, sweetheart. Now turn that frown upside down and try to enjoy the rest of the evening. There's so much to celebrate, Lily."

"You mean I can't call it a night and go hide out in my room?"

"If you do, I have a feeling you might regret it."

"What do you—"

He gently turned me, and a small whimper spilled out of me. Standing at the door in his groomsman tux was Kaiden.

"He's here."

"He's here." Dad's hand slipped down to the

small of my back and nudged me forward gently. "Just like I knew he would be. Go to him, Lily."

"I-I, yeah, okay."

Blood roared in my ears, my heart beating out of my chest as I crossed the room. Kaiden took a step forward, searching my eyes. "I am so fucking sorry," he rushed out at the same time as I blurted, "You're here."

"You didn't think I'd— Fuck, Lily. Come here." He pulled me into his arms and everything inside me went quiet and still.

Kaiden had always been my shelter. My constant.

"I will always come for you, Lily," he said. "Even if I have to take a little detour first." He pressed a kiss to my forehead as his fingers gently curved around the back of my neck.

My eyelashes fluttered as I gazed up at him. "I'm angry," I admitted.

"I know, babe. I'm angry too. But I'm here now and you look... Fuck, Lily, you look stunning. Dance with me?"

"You want to dance? But you just got here, and—"

"Dance with me, please."

All I could do was give him a small nod. I was too confused, too overwhelmed to even speak. Kaiden was here and it was all I wanted. But it didn't negate the anger and disappointment I felt.

My mind was an exhausting place to be sometimes but in Kaiden's arms, I always felt a little bit better.

And as he led me out to the dance floor, the walls I'd slowly been building around my heart began to crumble, piece by little piece.

CHAPTER TWENTY

KAIDEN

JASE GAVE me a subtle nod as I led his daughter into the middle of the dance floor and pulled her into my arms.

She looked gorgeous in the pale gold dress, the shimmering tone contrasting against her dark curls and sun-kissed skin. But it was imagining Lily in a white dress, the two of us about to have our first dance, that really hit me in the feels.

Fuck, I wanted that.

Her. Us. The big wedding.

I wanted to claim her as mine in front of our friends and family, to slide my wedding ring on her finger and listen to the officiant announce us as husband and wife.

But Avery and Cameron would kick my ass six ways to Sunday if I did something stupid like drop to my knee and propose. Not to mention the fact Lily would never forgive me for stealing Miley's thunder. So I pushed that thought to the back of my mind and focused on how fucking beautiful she looked.

"I'm sorry." I brushed my lips against her ears as she pressed in close. "I didn't know Coach would make us stay late. Then there was an accident on the highway, and then the plane out of Kansas City had been delayed. When I finally got in the air and they announced we had to divert because of a storm, I couldn't believe it."

"It doesn't matter," she said.

"Yeah, Lil." I pulled back to look her in the eye. "It does. I hate letting you down. I hate knowing that you think I put football above you when the truth is, I would survive if I lost football, but I wouldn't survive if I lost you."

"Kaiden." Her breath caught as she stared up at me with big uncertain eyes.

"I love you, Lily May Ford. I will always love you."

Lily didn't reply but she tucked her cheek into my chest and let me hold her as we danced.

When the song finished, and the DJ changed the

tempo to something more upbeat we broke apart. "We should probably talk," I said.

"Later. You're here now, that's all that matters."

Our friends swarmed us, wrapping me and Lily in a group hug. "Knew you'd make it," Aaron grinned.

"It's good to see you," Ezra added.

"Ease up, yeah. You're crushing Lily."

"It's fine." Her soft laughter was like music to my fucking ears.

"Got you a beer for your troubles," Bryan handed me the bottle.

"Thanks." Looping my arm around Lily's waist, I tucked her to my side as we moved to the edge of the dance floor.

"They look happy." Avery caught my eye over Miley's shoulder, and I raised my beer, mouthing, "Congratulations."

Fuck, I wanted that.

I wanted all eyes on me as I danced with my wife. But I didn't want to get it wrong, not after waiting so long.

Until Aaron opened his big stupid mouth. "You know, Miley still has to throw the bouquet." His amused gaze settled right on me.

"You know Poppy will make sure she catches that shit," Ezra said.

"You know it." She beamed at Aaron, but he didn't look worried, not one bit.

"You think your dad will kick my ass if I get down on one knee tonight?"

"You shouldn't joke about things like that," Sofia said.

"Who said I'm joking?" A knowing glint lit up his eyes and dread curdled in my stomach. If he did it... No, he wouldn't.

Not tonight, of all the nights.

I tried to push my worries and doubts to one side. After the journey from hell, I'd made it. That's all that mattered.

Lily and I could enjoy a night with our friends and family and then we could talk.

And if she didn't want to talk, then she could listen.

Because I sure had plenty to say to her.

LILY

Somewhere between Kaiden arriving and my fourth or fifth glass of champagne, I decided I was having the best night ever.

"He can't take his eyes off you," Ashleigh said with a sloppy grin.

We were all a little tipsy. But there was a lot to celebrate.

Avery and Miley were married.

Married.

My cousin was all grown up. River was getting stronger by the day and Peyton and Xander hoped she would be taken off all the machines soon. Bryan was about to start his new job at the high school. Cole and Sofia were getting ready for another trip. Kaiden's dream of playing in the NFL was about to come true.

Everyone had a reason to be happy.

"He's drunk," I said.

"I don't think so. He only had like three beers."

"Don't be silly. They're all drunk. Look at Aaron and his dad."

We watched the two of them try to pull off some strange dance moves, the crowd cheering them on.

Of course the Bennets would be the life and soul of the party, my sister not far behind them. Laughter bubbled in my chest. They looked so ridiculous, but they were having fun.

I envied them. I'd never been carefree or reckless. Because life had taught me from a young age that people could be cruel. They could be cruel and dishonest and downright mean. But Kaiden had shown me that it didn't always have to be that way.

He'd shown me that it was okay to let people in. To trust them.

He'd done that.

His patience with me back then had been admirable. I wasn't always an easy person to love, but he made it look effortless.

"Oh, oh, he's coming over here." Ashleigh grinned.

Before I could turn around, strong arms slid around my waist and Kaiden's breath tickled the back of my neck. "You're killing me here, Lil," he said in a husky voice.

"I'm only dancing," I chuckled, folding my arms over his, loving how strong and safe he made me feel.

"It's been two weeks, babe. Two weeks since I got to taste you. Two whole weeks since I felt you clenched around me."

"Kaiden," my breath hitched, shivers rippling down my spine.

"Two weeks and every day has been torture." He pulled me closer, letting me feel the evidence of his desire. "I love you, Lily Ford. I love you so fucking much."

I turned in his arms, desperate to see him. Desperate to look him in the eye and feel his mouth on mine. Winding my arms around the back of his neck, I crushed us together.

"Is my girl drunk?" He grinned, and I nodded. "A little."

"Good. You deserve to enjoy yourself, Lily. But it makes me feel a hell of a lot better knowing I'll be here to look after you."

"I'm not *that* drunk."

"Good, because I wouldn't feel right taking advantage of you. I want you to be fully aware of all the things I plan to do to you later."

I sucked in another shaky breath. "When can we leave?"

His deep laughter rumbled through me. "Soon." He dropped a kiss on my head. "But first, I want to dance with my girl again."

I smiled up at him, ignoring every little doubt and insecurity. Because Kaiden was here. He was here and I was going to soak up every second with him.

"What do you say, babe? Dance with me again?"

My smile grew, my heart fluttering in my chest as I let out a contented sigh.

"I think that can be arranged."

"I can't believe you caught the bouquet," Poppy complained as we headed up to our rooms.

"Here, you have it." I thrust it at her, earning me a round of laughs from the guys.

"No, that's not—"

"Just take it, babe." Aaron hugged her close. "We all know I'm going to put a ring on your finger soon anyway."

"Aaron! You can't say stuff like that."

"Why not? It's true."

The two of them started bickering so Kaiden and I dropped back a little, giving them space.

"You didn't have to give that to her, you know."

"It doesn't matter." I shrugged.

The wedding reception had been a blast. I hadn't expected to enjoy myself quite so much but once Kaiden showed up, it was like everything in my world felt right again. We'd danced and laughed, and I drank one too many glasses of champagne. It felt good, I felt good.

But every step toward our room, the illusion began to slip.

Because come Tuesday, he would return to Kansas.

Without me.

"Hey, what's wrong?"

"Nothing." I forced a smile onto my lips. "Tonight has been a good night."

"I'm just glad I made it and got to see you in this dress," he said. "Come on, this is us." He steered me toward the door, the keycard already in his hand.

"Night guys," Poppy called from down the hall. We waved but Aaron had my sister pinned up against the wall, kissing the crap out of her.

"They couldn't wait to get in their room?" I murmured, and Kaiden chuckled as he led me inside.

The air seemed to thin and stretch between us as I turned and Kaiden watched me from where he leaned up against the door.

"What?"

"Nothing." He shook his head a little as if he was physically dismissing whatever he'd been thinking.

"Tell me," I urged, taking a step toward him.

"I can't."

"Can't or won't?"

There were things we needed to talk about still. Important things. But I was stuck on his expression as he'd watched me just now. The intensity churning in his eyes. Kaiden had been about to say something, something I wanted to hear.

Something I needed to hear.

"It doesn't matter," he said quietly.

"I think it does." I took another step toward him,

the champagne still coursing through my veins, giving me a false sense of confidence.

Sliding my hand around my neck, I gently pulled the halter ribbon free, letting the soft material fall down my body.

"Fuck," Kaiden breathed, not taking his eyes off me. "You're not playing fair."

"Tell me what you were going to say."

"Lily." He sounded pained.

"Tell me..."

"I nearly did something really fucking stupid tonight," he finally confessed, closing the distance between us.

"I-I don't understand."

What was he saying?

What did he mean?

Suddenly, Kaiden dropped to his knees before me and shaped my waist with his hands. "I wanted to do it, Lily. I wanted to do it so fucking badly."

"Kaiden, what are you—" It hit me then. A moment of heart stopping clarity. "Oh my God." I clapped my hand over my mouth.

"But I didn't do it. Because I didn't want you to think it was an apology proposal. I didn't want to steal Avery and Miley's thunder, and I didn't want your dad—"

"Stop, just... stop." I inhaled a shuddering breath,

hardly able to believe what was happening. "Kaiden, I'm drunk. I'm drunk and half-naked and you're on your knees looking at me like you're still about to do something stupid."

"Because I think I might be." His mouth quirked, a boyish sparkle in his eyes. "I wanted it to be perfect. I had planned the perfect night but then Peyton went into labor, and you were so worried, I couldn't do it. So I told myself I'd wait. For another perfect moment. But Lily, I don't need perfect. I just need you, babe. Today. Tomorrow. And every day after that.

"I know you're scared about what will happen when we move to Kansas. But you have nothing to worry about. I love you." He reached for my hand, twining our fingers together. "I love you so fucking much, babe. I want you by my side and in my bed. I want you wearing my number on game days, cheering me on from the crowd. I want us to have a life together. A family. I want it all, Lily. And I only want it with you."

Tears rolled down my cheeks as his words sank into me. They wrapped around my heart and smoothed some of the cracks. Kaiden loved me. I'd never doubted that. He was right though, I was scared. Terrified of my own mind and my own insecurities. But I also knew without a shadow of a doubt, I loved Kaiden, and I wanted everything he'd just described.

"Ask me," I said.

"Lily, maybe it's not—"

"Ask me, Kaiden." I smiled, and for the first time since he'd left, I finally felt like maybe everything would be okay.

"Lily, I think I have loved you since the moment we went into Lindsey Filmer's boat shed and I kissed you. Your inner strength amazes me. Your kind heart and sense of loyalty. Your beautiful smile and addictive laugh. It's you, Lily. It was you then. It was you today. And it will be you until my very last breath.

"Will you, Lily May Ford, grow old with me? Will you live and laugh and love with me? Will you be mine always? Will you marry me?"

"Yes, Kaiden." I dropped to my knees and threw my arms around him.

My rock.

My heart.

My *home*.

"Yes, I'll marry you."

CHAPTER TWENTY-ONE

KAIDEN

"IT'S SO BEAUTIFUL," Lily let out a contented sigh as she flexed her fingers, the princess cut ring now sitting on her ring finger glinting in the soft light of the lamp.

She was naked, we both were, the sheet strewn around us.

After I'd proposed and she'd said yes, I'd dug the ring out of my overnight bag, slid it onto her finger, and then showed her just exactly how much I loved her.

Twice.

It was late now. Really fucking late. But I didn't want to close my eyes and go to sleep in case this was all a dream. Or in case, she woke up and changed her mind.

"Mrs. Lily Thatcher," I said, kissing her shoulder as I ran my hand up her stomach, cupping one of her breasts. "I like the sound of that."

"Is this real? It doesn't feel real," she said.

"Oh, it's real." I slid my fingers between hers, interlocking our hands. "You're mine now."

"You know, we still need to talk about some things."

"I know. But first, I want to show you something." Kissing her shoulder again, I slipped out of the bed and grabbed my cell phone.

When I got back in, I sat up against the headboard and pulled Lily to my side. "Check this out." I opened the webpage and waited for it to load.

"What is it?" Her brows furrowed as she waited.

"Look."

"It's an apartment."

"I know." I smiled. "It's in a good location. I made some inquiries on the ride over and there's a couple of empty units. Master suite. The building has a rooftop terrace. Swimming pool. Gym."

"Fancy."

"I was thinking you could fly out in a couple of weeks, and we could check it out. Maybe submit your résumé to a few places while we're there."

"You've really given this some thought." She gazed up at me.

"Lily, it's all I think about. You, me, our life together."

"I thought…" She trailed off, inhaling a shuddering breath.

"I know. And I'm sorry I waited so long. But I'd think about doing it and then get all up in my head. Worrying that you might think we were rushing or that it wasn't the right time. Then I was going to do it and Peyton went into labor. It felt like an omen.

"I guess it doesn't matter now." She held up her left hand again.

"No, I guess it doesn't. How do you feel about a winter wedding?" I asked.

"This winter?" She glanced up at me, and I nodded.

"I don't want to wait any longer than I have to."

"This winter might be a bit soon. I'll barely be settled into our new place, a new job. Next spring?"

"Next spring it is."

"But I want to get married in Rixon."

"I assumed we would."

"And what else have you assumed?" The playful lilt in her voice settled the nervous energy still zipping through me.

Lily had said yes. She was wearing my ring. But I

could still feel her hesitation.

I didn't blame her. The last two weeks—longer than that really—had been strained. A distance there between us that our doubts and fears had played into. But what she still didn't realize was that she wasn't the only one who felt it.

"I've always thought we'd get married in your parents' yard. Hire a big marquee and let your mom and aunt Hailee do their thing.

"We'd keep it low-key because we don't need everyone and their grandma there. Just our nearest and dearest. The people most important in our lives."

"It sounds perfect," she said with a soft sigh.

"It will be perfect," I corrected. "This ring isn't an apology or a Band-Aid, Lily. It's a promise. A promise that I'm yours and you're mine and no distance or time apart will ever change that."

"You really are saying all the right things tonight." She chuckled, sliding her hand up my chest and tucking herself closer.

"Because it's important to me that you know the truth." I kissed her head, wanting to do a lot more than that. But it was late, and we had breakfast with everyone in the morning.

A thought hit me then.

One I wasn't sure I wanted the answer to.

"Tomorrow morning... what do you want to tell

everyone?"

"What do you mean?"

"Well, do you want to wait to tell everyone?"

God, if she wanted to wait it would crush me. But I'd do it. I'd do it for her.

"No, I don't want to wait. Why would you think that?"

"I don't know." I lifted my shoulder in a small shrug. "I guess I just thought—"

Lily climbed onto my lap, looping her arms around my neck. "I want to tell them, Kaiden."

"Yeah?" I swallowed hard.

"Mm-hmm." Her lips curved. "I love you and I want to spend the rest of my life with you. That is all I've wanted for a long time now."

"You want to spend the rest of your life with me, Lil?"

"I do."

I sat up, banding my arm around her waist and crushing her chest to mine. She stared at me with such intensity it made my heart ratchet and my head spin.

Lily was mine.

Tonight.

Tomorrow.

Forever.

If the ring on her finger didn't confirm that, the

love and adoration in her eyes did.

POPPY

Breakfast was a fairly quiet affair, everyone a little hungover from the night before.

The wedding had been perfect, but we'd all stayed and partied long after we'd waved Avery and Miley off. They were headed off on their honeymoon courtesy of all our parents who had chipped in to get them a suite at a five-star resort in Aruba.

"Any sign of Lily and Kaiden yet?" Dad asked.

"Not yet."

"They seemed okay last night though, right?"

"Yeah, Dad, they seemed okay." Lily had been a little tipsy, but she'd been smiling, and they had danced together a lot. So I figured that they had smoothed things over.

At least, I hoped they had because I didn't like seeing my sister sad.

"Look what the cat dragged in," Dad chuckled as Asher joined us.

"I think something crawled inside me and died."

"We're not twenty-one anymore, Ash." Mya rolled her eyes. "You can't keep up with the kids."

He dropped down onto a chair and ran a hand down his face. "I'll have you know I drank *the kids* under the table." His weary gaze flicked toward Aaron and Ezra who both smirked.

"We were up at eight and down here at nine, old man."

"They have a point, Ash," Mya said, fighting a grin.

"Oh hush, woman, and get me some coffee. Strong, black coffee." He dropped his head on the table, and everyone laughed.

"I think you broke him," I said to Aaron and Ezra.

"He only got what he deserved. Oh, here's Lily and Kaiden."

I glanced around and sure enough my sister and Kaiden headed toward us.

"What do you call this?" Aaron said. "We've all been— Back the fuck up." His eyes went wide. "What is that?"

"What is— *Lily?*" I gawked at her. At the giant freaking rock on her ring finger.

"Surprise," she said meekly, practically burying herself into Kaiden's side. "We kind of got engaged last night."

"Oh my God." I jumped out of my seat and went to her. "Let me see that." Taking her hand in mine I admired the ring. "Your boy did good." I smiled at Kaiden. "Congratulations, I'm so happy for you."

Lily hugged me back. "Thank you, for everything."

"I'd say I told you so, but I don't want to ruin the moment."

She pulled back, giving me a bemused smile. There wasn't any more time to talk because our family and friends all descended, wanting to congratulate them.

"So much for not proposing at a wedding," Aaron muttered.

"I didn't plan on doing it," Kaiden said. "It just happened."

"He didn't even have the ring."

"What the hell do you mean, he didn't have the ring?" Dad came over.

"Like I said, it just happened."

"My daughter deserved a proper proposal, son. A big grand gesture."

"It was perfect, Dad."

"Doesn't sound perfect to me if he didn't even have the ring. You don't need to settle, Lil. You don't need—"

"Jase." Mom shook her head. "Back off. This is all we wanted, remember."

"I'm only busting his balls." Dad's expression melted into a grin. "I'm happy for you, son. About time you grew a pair and popped the question."

"You knew?" Lily stared at Dad.

"We may have talked about it."

"Oh."

Kaiden leaned down and brushed a kiss to Lily's cheek, whispering something to her. Whatever it was, it made her blush.

"Can we eat now?" Kaiden asked. "We're starving."

"I bet you are." Aaron grinned and I elbowed him in the ribs.

"Behave."

"What? I'm just saying, I bet they worked up quite the appetite."

"Enough of that." Dad glowered at him, nudging Lily and Kaiden away from the rest of us.

We all sat down again but I kept one eye on them, smiling at the pride written all over Dad's face. All he'd ever wanted was to see me and Lily happy and content.

He pulled Lily into his arms, hugging her tightly before moving to Kaiden. Emotion lodged into my throat, and Aaron squeezed my knee. "Are you crying?"

"No, I'm not." I poked my tongue out at him. "I'm just really happy for them."

"Yeah, if anyone deserves it, it's Lily and Kaiden."

"You'd better step up now, Son," Asher said.

"Dad, come on."

"What? I'm just saying. Kaiden has set the precedent now. The rest of you need to pull your heads out and—"

"You need to eat. Put something in that delicate stomach of yours," Mya said, giving me an apologetic look. But I didn't mind, I was used to the Bennet men by now.

Lily and Kaiden joined us, and Dad went to sit with Mom.

"I can't believe you waited all these years and then popped the question without the ring," Gav said. "Only you, Thatcher. Only you."

Kaiden flipped him off. "I had the ring, asshole. I just didn't have it on me at that precise moment."

"Have you thought about the wedding?" Ashleigh asked.

"Leigh, it's been a few hours."

"When we make any plans, you'll all be the first to know." Kaiden smiled down at my sister, and I saw it.

The tiny white lie.

They'd probably stayed up half the night planning their dream wedding. I bet they'd even gone so far as to write the guest list.

But I didn't call them out on it. This was their moment, and they deserved it.

"Maybe we should have a wedding schedule," Aaron suggested.

"I have got to hear this," Ezra murmured.

"Well, we all managed to get to Rixon for Miley and Avery's big day. There's like seven couples. If we each take a year, it'll mean at least one guaranteed reunion every—"

"Seriously, Poppy," Cole said. "How do you put up with his shit?"

"He's an excellent—"

"Poppy June Ford," Dad groaned. "I know you're not about to say what I think you're about to say."

"He's an excellent cook." I shrugged, flashing my dad a little smirk.

"I'm sure he is. But I'd prefer to hear less about it over breakfast."

"Sorry, Jase," Aaron piped up. "Can't take these kids anywhere."

Laughter broke out again, and I soaked it up.

Our lives were changing, moving in different directions, and pulling us apart. But one thing would always remain.

We'd always be family.

And no amount of time or space would ever change that.

CHAPTER TWENTY-TWO

XANDER

"I HEAR CONGRATULATIONS ARE IN ORDER," I said as Lily and Kaiden came into River's room.

She'd been given her own space now she was off most of the machines helping her breathe and regulate her body temperature.

"Thanks," Kaiden said, keeping one hand on his fiancée.

Fuck. The pressure was on now. Once one guy in a friend group proposed the rest usually fell like dominoes. But we had our hands full with River. Weddings and all that other stuff could wait.

Peyton knew I loved her.

I didn't need to put a ring on her finger to prove that.

"How's she doing?" he asked, tipping his head toward where River slept peacefully.

"She's a fighter."

"She's growing," Lily said, going over to the bassinet.

"Yeah, she's gained a few more ounces."

"Where's Peyton?"

"She'll be—"

The door opened and Peyton came inside.

"You're here." She smiled. "Let me see."

Lily held out her hand and the two of them gushed over the rather impressive ring on her finger.

"That signing bonus must have been pretty nice." I teased.

"Asshole." Kaiden pulled a chair over and sat down beside me. "You missed a good day."

"I couldn't leave them, it didn't feel right."

Peyton had tried to persuade me to go. Avery was my nephew, after all. But I'd seen the disappointment in her eyes, the hurt. No way was I going to leave my girls.

"I get it," he said. "We all do. How is she doing?"

I knew he didn't mean River.

"She's better. Still finding it hard but we'll get there." I watched Peyton and Lily coo and fuss over

River. "You going to tell me about stealing Avery's thunder or what?"

"Come on, man. It wasn't even like that." His lips twisted a little.

"You almost missed the wedding and needed a really big apology gesture?"

"Fuck you, Chase. Fuck. You." Laughter crinkled his eyes. "I almost did it, you know. The night Peyton went into labor, I had the whole thing planned."

"Fuck, I didn't realize."

"Yeah, fuck." He sat back in the chair, eyes fixed on Lily. "Then I had to leave her, and everything felt... wrong."

"You haven't liked being in Kansas with the team?"

"The team's great. Football is... it's my life. But Lily is my heart, Xan. None of it means anything if I don't have her by my side."

"Yeah." I gazed at my girls. The woman I loved more than anything and the daughter I wasn't sure I deserved. "I know exactly what you mean. So what's the plan?"

"We're looking at apartments in a couple of weeks. I found a place, looks kind of perfect."

"I'm happy for you. Both of you."

"Is it weird, watching all of us grow up?"

"Fuck you." I smirked. "I'm not that much older

than you are." Nearly ten years, but who was counting.

"Whatever you say, old man." He got up, squeezing my shoulder as he passed to get to the girls. "Whatever you say."

"So, did anyone embarrass themselves at the wedding reception?" I asked sometime later.

"Asher and Aaron made a spectacle of themselves," Lily said, and I chuckled.

"Why am I not surprised."

Kaiden snorted. "Ash didn't look so good this morning at breakfast, that was for sure."

"Was the first dance beautiful?" Peyton asked.

"Yeah. My dad made me dance with him until Kaiden showed up."

"Smooth entrance." I smirked.

"Something like that."

"I still can't believe you're engaged," Peyton let out a dreamy sigh as River slept peacefully in her arms. "I've only been waiting like forever for this."

"Tell me about it." Lily gave Kaiden a teasing glance.

"You're never going to let me live this down, are you?"

"Oh, I don't know. I might, one day."

"Okay, lovebirds, let's cool it. Baby present," I said.

"She's going to make the cutest flower girl." Lily smiled.

"For real, you want..."

"Of course. She's my first niece. She has to be in the wedding. Especially if her mama is going to be my bridesmaid."

Peyton let out a little squeal of delight but quickly covered her mouth. "Oops."

"Here, let me take her," I said, scooping River out of her mom's arms.

"Now who's the smooth one," Kaiden said.

"You want to take her? It'll be good practice for the future."

"Oh no," Lily blurted, cheeks turning bright red. "We're not in any rush."

"You say that now but wait until she's coming for sleepovers with her aunt Lily and uncle Kaiden."

"Babysitting is the best form of contraception, no?" Kaiden fought a smile.

"We can't wait to look after her." Lily's whole face lit up but then her expression fell.

"Lil, what is it?"

"I'm going to miss out on so much."

"Oh, babe. You can't think like that. It's Kansas, not the end of the earth. We'll visit all the time, and we can video call and send you email updates."

"You promise?"

"Of course I do," Peyton said. "You'll be a part of River's life no matter where you are."

Lily nodded, and Kaiden leaned over to grab her hand. "Two bedrooms. We'll only look at apartments with two bedrooms. That way we can have a guest room for when everyone visits."

"Okay."

"See," Peyton added, sensing the tension. "You're not going to get rid of us that easily. We're family, Lil. Nothing will ever change that."

PEYTON

"You good?" Xander asked as I got comfortable in the chair ready to feed River.

"I'm okay." I smiled at him and then at our daughter. "She seems bigger today."

"She'll only get stronger and bigger from here on out. You heard what the doctor said, she's a fighter."

"I just love her so much, Xander."

"I know, babe. I know."

"Lily seemed happier."

"Maybe she just needed to know Kaiden was all in."

"I think deep down, she knew that. But sometimes she struggles to keep a levelhead."

"Don't we all," he murmured.

"Xander Chase, are you admitting that you get scared sometimes too?"

"Hands down the scariest moment of my life when you went into early labor. The thought of losing you or her..."

"Shh." I reached for his hand. "We're both going to be fine."

"I'm probably going to be an overbearing ass, you know that, right?" His mouth quirked.

"I would expect nothing less. Lily said she could see me in her today."

"Oh, she's all her mama."

"I don't know. Sometimes I look at her and see you."

"She's the most beautiful baby I've ever seen. She's all you, Peyton."

"Sometimes you really do say the sweetest things." I flashed him a playful smile. "This is nice. It almost feels like we're doing it for real now she has her own room."

"Babe, we are doing it for real. Just because she isn't home with us yet doesn't change anything."

"I know, I just feel like we're missing out on so much."

My heart was still so heavy, but I was trying to be more upbeat. River was doing amazing, and they were talking about discharging her soon.

I just wanted to be out of here, at home with her and Xander.

"Soon, babe." He brushed his thumb over the back of my hand. "I love you both, so fucking much."

"Xander!" I chided. "Little ears present."

"She doesn't know what I'm saying." Laughter rumbled in his chest.

"You say that now, but when her first word is a cuss word..."

"Fine, fine. I'll try and stop. But I can't make any promises." His expression turned serious, and I frowned.

"What is it?"

"I'll forever be in awe of you, Peyton, you know that, right?"

"Xander..."

"No, let me get this out. You've given me so much. I promise I will always do right by you and River. And if I don't, you have my full permission to kick my ass."

"Pretty sure Jase will do that for me." I laughed, despite the emotion lodged in my throat.

"Yeah, you're probably right. He loves you like his own."

"I know."

And I did.

I might not have been family by blood, but I was family. Jason and Felicity had never made me feel anything less. And I was so thankful that River would grow up around such a big and loving group of people.

Some of the best people I knew.

Because at the end of the day, that's all anyone wanted. To have a place on this earth. To be loved and cherished and valued.

And I would spend every second of every day making sure my daughter knew that.

But that sentiment felt bittersweet after seeing Lily and Kaiden earlier.

"Does it make me a horrible person that I wish Lily didn't have to leave?" I said.

"I did wonder if that little speech earlier was for her benefit only."

"She's nervous, it's understandable. Moving to a new town where she doesn't know anyone."

"But life can't always be about standing still. Look at me. I left Rixon and moved to Halston because I knew I couldn't grow there."

"You left because you were running from your problems."

"That too," he conceded. "But there's nothing wrong with giving yourself time and space. If we never push ourselves to face our fears, we can never move forward.

"Moving to Kansas with Kaiden will be a good thing," he said. "She'll still have you all in her corner, but it'll give her an opportunity to grow."

"Yeah, I think it'll be a good thing for her too. I'll just miss her."

Lily was my person. She'd been my person for as long as I could remember. Kansas felt so far away. But Xander had a point.

"We'll visit them, right?"

"Of course we will." His eyes held a thousand promises. "And Lily will come home. That's the beauty of moving away. You always get to come home."

"You're my home," I said. "You and River." My heart was so full of love I thought it might explode.

"Who do you think will drop next?" Xander changed the subject.

"Drop... Oh," I chuckled. "My bet is Aaron or Bryan."

"With McKay and Cole following closely behind."

"Something like that. Aaron has probably started a wager."

"He and Poppy are a match made in heaven."

"Yep." I grinned. "Next couple to get pregnant?"

"Come on, babe. I don't—"

"I think it'll be Ashleigh and Ezra."

"You think? I would have said McKay and Pen. They've got that whole younger sibling thing working for them."

"Thought you didn't want to play this game."

"Haven't you realized by now, there isn't much I wouldn't do for you."

"You hear that, my sweet baby girl," I stroked River's cheek. "We have your daddy wrapped around our fingers. He's going to be in so much trouble, isn't he."

"You're worth it," he said, looking at us both with so much love and affection I felt like a giddy schoolgirl, falling in love with him all over again.

"You know, I never thought I'd have this."

"Then we can be grateful together."

"We can."

Because we had something special.

Something rare and precious.

Something I would never ever take for granted.

CHAPTER TWENTY-THREE

LILY

"I STILL CAN'T BELIEVE you were about to propose."

"Yep. Had the ring ready and everything. Even the server was in on it. But the second you got the call, I knew it wasn't going to happen."

"Kaiden, I'm so sorry."

"Shh." He grabbed my hand and tugged me into his chest as we walked toward my house.

We'd had our do-over tonight.

A romantic meal at The Nook. Same table. Same beautiful setting. Only this time, he didn't have the ring in his pocket because it was on my finger.

Despite all the reservations I had about moving

to Kansas, the lingering doubts, I was floating on cloud nine.

Engaged.

We were *engaged*.

And I didn't know how much it would mean to me until Kaiden had dropped to his knees before me and poured his heart out.

"It doesn't matter now," he said, kissing my forehead. "All that matters is this. Us. And the life we're going to create together. Now can we please go inside. I have big plans for you."

A shiver went down my spine at the huskiness in his voice as we reached the front door.

Mom and Dad were out tonight, and Poppy was staying over at the Bennets' house which meant we had the house to ourselves for a few hours. Something I was dying to take advantage of since Kaiden would leave again on Tuesday.

But I didn't want to dwell on that.

Not tonight.

Not when I was so happy and—

"Surprise!" Our family and friends were crammed into the hall, a homemade banner hanging on the wall.

"What is—"

"We wanted to surprise you." Poppy beamed.

"Oh, I'm surprised," I said, glancing back at Kaiden. "Did you know about this?"

"Nope, I'm as surprised as you."

I saw a flash of disappointment in his eyes.

We'd both been looking forward to being home alone.

"Oh, turn those frowns upside down," Aaron said. "You can still get freaky later. You'll just have to keep—"

"Oh my God, Aaron." Poppy clapped her hand over his mouth. "We're sorry for hijacking your romantic night together but Sofia and Cole leave tomorrow, and we wanted to celebrate your happy news."

"It was very thoughtful of you. All of you," I said.

"Even if we cockbl—"

"Ash, seriously, deal with your son or I will," Dad grumbled. "Come on, we've got the grill on and the steaks aren't going to cook themselves."

The yard was full of our closest friends and family. It was perfect. Even if it meant putting our plans on hold.

"You good?" Kaiden ran his nose along the back of my neck, pressing a kiss to my shoulder.

"Yeah. I was disappointed at first, but this is kind of nice. Having everyone here. Although it's a shame Peyton and—"

Kaiden gently gripped my chin and turned my head over to the back door.

"Oh my God." I got up and rushed over to Peyton and Xander. "What are you doing here?"

"I didn't want to miss this too," Peyton said, hugging me. "Congratulations. Again. I'm so unbelievably happy for you both."

"I can't believe you're here. What about River?"

"She's fine. Sleeping. We'll only stay an hour. Then head back to check on her."

"She's in good hands," Xander said. "And besides, I thought it would do this one good to have an hour of normal." He dropped a kiss on Peyton's head and said, "I'm going to find the men and do manly things."

"Follow the plume of smoke," I said.

Dad had taken up residence at the grill, keeping the supply of burgers and steaks flowing.

"Lily," my best friend said. "You're glowing."

"I feel different. I know that sounds silly, Pey, but I do."

"You weren't upset they ruined your romantic night with your fiancé?" She waggled her brows.

"I can't deny I was a tad disappointed. Especially since he goes back Tuesday. But this, having everyone here, it's worth it."

"Besides, from the way he's looking at you," she said, "I think there's still hope for you yet."

"Peyton." I flushed all over. But when I glanced over at Kaiden, I realized she was right.

He was making no attempt to hide the hunger in his gaze.

"God, I remember that feeling."

"Oh, hush. You're like the world's hottest mom. Xander still looks at you like that."

"Oh, I know he does. But I think I'm broken... down there." She grimaced. "I can't ever imagine letting him anywhere near me again."

"You will. Once things heal and you get River home."

"What if it's different? What if he doesn't like my body anymore?"

I looked at her, *really* looked at her. My best friend. The girl I'd spent most of my teenage years so envious of.

Peyton was always so beautiful and confident and fearless. I'd wanted to be more like her. There were times when I still did.

But Peyton was human just like the rest of us. She still had fears and doubts and insecurities.

"Come here." I pulled her into my arms. "Xander loves you, babe. He loves you so much. And after watching you give birth to his daughter and handle everything like a pro, I'm sure he loves you more than ever."

"You think?" She eased back to look me in the eye.

"I know." I smiled. "You gave him one of the greatest gifts you could. Don't ever doubt the power in that."

"Okay, I need a drink. This was supposed to be an hour of good old-fashioned, normal fun and I'm already crying." She swiped the tears from her eyes. "These damn hormones won't stop."

"I'm glad you're here, Peyton."

"Me too, Lil. Me too."

KAIDEN

"How badly do you want to tell everyone to fuck off so you can take Lily upstairs?" Aaron said with a knowing smirk.

"We're not all sex-obsessed like you and Poppy."

"Speak for yourself, Thatch," Gav said. "Millie is a regular little cockblocker. Same with Max. We're constantly having to find ways to sneak some one-on-one time."

"You could try, I don't know... getting your own place." Bryan chuckled.

"Asshole. You know it's not that simple. We have to think about the kids."

"Sorry, I didn't mean to be a dick. I know it's not easy."

"It's all good. But some of us have responsibilities."

"We get it," I said. "But one day you're going to have to put yourself first."

"Yeah, we'll see." He got a faraway look in his eyes, like he couldn't imagine a time where he and Pen didn't have to help raise their kid brother and sister.

"Well, when me and Lily get settled, you're all invited to come and visit us."

"Does that invitation come with VIP tickets to your first game?"

"Don't get ahead of yourself. I might not even make the roster yet."

"You'll make it." Bryan gave me a reassuring nod.

"Only time will tell."

I didn't want to think too far ahead. All I could do was apply the mantra that had gotten me through four years of college football. Play hard. Fight hard. And hope like hell it was enough.

"It's hard to think that in another four years, we'll all be in the next stage of our lives," Cole said. "Weddings, kids, careers."

"You got something you want to tell us, Kandon?" Aaron arched his brow.

"Don't look at me. Me and Sofia have no plans to put down roots yet. Too much we want to see and do."

"Vera won't last forever," he said.

"She's still got plenty of miles left in her yet."

"What about you, E? Reckon you'll end up playing opposite this one next year?"

"I'm not getting ahead of myself."

"You've got this," I said.

Ezra wasn't just good—he was really fucking good. But he didn't want it the way I always had growing up.

"What about you, Thatch?" Bryan said. "First comes love, then comes marriage, then comes the baby in a baby carriage."

"Fucking idiot," I muttered.

"Yeah, but you want that, right? You want it all with her?"

"Dude, this is Kaiden we're talking about," Gav

tsked. "He wouldn't have put a ring on it if he didn't want it."

"I want it." I glanced over to where Lily was talking to the girls. She looked so beautiful, so fucking happy my chest swelled with pride.

"I give it six months," Aaron announced. "Six months and you'll have a baby inside her."

I didn't even deny it. Because given half the chance, I'd jump ahead to all that stuff.

The wedding, a family. Brown-haired, blue-eyed little babies who looked just like their mom.

We were still young, yeah. But I knew. In my soul, I knew Lily was it for me.

She had been ever since I walked into that boat shed with her.

"I thought they would never leave," I said as Lily slipped into bed beside me.

She nestled into my side, laying her palm against my chest. "Tonight was fun."

"It was. But I missed you."

"I was right there."

"I know. But I like having you close by. I like being able to touch you." I ran a hand down her spine, gently squeezing her ass. "I had so many plans for tonight."

"Tell me..."

"Well, first I was going to strip you naked and kiss every inch of your—"

"Night, kids." A loud knock rattled the door. "If you need anything—"

"We got it, Dad," Lily yelled back.

"Okay, sweetheart. Me and your mom are going to bed now. We'll see you in the morning. Maybe we can—"

"Dad!"

His laughter echoed through the door, and Lily buried her face in my chest with a groan. "He's insufferable."

"He's... something."

No way I could finish what I'd just started now, knowing Jase was probably out there, stalking the hallway.

I let out a heavy sigh. "Tomorrow night I'm checking us into a hotel."

"What? Why?"

Nudging Lily onto her back, I leaned over her. "Because I want some alone time with my fiancée and her gorgeous, tempting body."

She reached for me, laying her hand against my cheek. "I love you, Kaiden. So much."

"I love you too." I turned my face to kiss her palm.

"We can be quiet." She gave me a coy smile.

"I don't want you quiet, Lil. Not when I fuck you the way I want to."

"Kaiden." Her breath caught, a streak of pink staining down her cheeks and down her neck. I dipped my head, kissing the soft skin there.

"But I'm not sure I can wait," I murmured. "Tonight has been torture."

"Tell me about it. The way you watched me..."

"All I could think about was stealing you away."

"I'm not sure my dad would have appreciated that."

"He's going to have to get used to it, Lil. You're mine now. This ring"—I touched her finger—"says so."

"He trusts you with my heart, you know. I wouldn't be lying here if he didn't."

"I know. And I'll always strive to be the kind of guy he's proud to call his future son-in-law."

"That sounds so weird." A faint smile traced her mouth as she looped her arms around my neck and pulled me down, our lips hovering.

"What are you doing?"

"I've changed my mind," she said. "I think I can be quiet."

"Oh yeah?"

Lily nodded, her smile turning playful and full of mischief. I brushed my mouth over hers, kissing her deeply.

My love for this woman knew no bounds. I felt it every time she looked at me, every time our lips met.

She was my endgame.

My forever goal.

And I couldn't wait until the day she walked down the aisle toward me and became my *wife*.

EPILOGUE

LILY

"AUNT LIL LIL." River fussed with the curls falling around my face.

"Oh no, Lil. Don't let her do that. You'll ruin your hair." Peyton took her daughter from me and handed her to Mom. "No more cuddles for the bride."

"Come on, she's so cute when she calls me Aunt Lil Lil, I can't resist."

"Peyton's right, sweetheart. It's almost time. We can't afford any hair or makeup disasters now."

"Fine. Steal the cutie."

"Did somebody say cutie?" Miley came into the room carrying a very animated Dexter.

I got up and went to them. "Did somebody wake up full of beans?"

"He sure did. I'm just about to hand him off to my mom before the ceremony. But I knew you wanted to see him."

"Of course I want to see him." I squeezed his pudgy little hand. "You be a good boy for grandma, okay? And we'll have a dance later." I kissed his soft baby hair, my heart fluttering.

Miley had been pregnant on her wedding day, but it wasn't meant to be. She'd miscarried at nine weeks. They had spent the next two years trying and just when they were about to start looking into their options, Dexter came along and surprised everyone.

"Good luck out there," Miley said. "Not that you need it. This day has been a long time coming."

Three years to the day in fact.

After Kaiden had proposed we had every intention of having a spring wedding, but life got in the way.

His first season with the Wild had turned into something neither of us had expected. Kaiden stepped in for their injured quarterback and earned himself the title of the NFLPA's number one rising star.

Life got pretty crazy after that.

But through it all, our relationship only went

from strength to strength. I found a job I loved. I made friends. Pushed myself to have new experiences. We hung out with a few guys from the team and their wives and girlfriends.

We built a life in Kansas.

We built a home.

A home that was about to become bigger thanks to the three positive pregnancy tests I'd taken just the other day.

I hadn't told Kaiden yet. It was his wedding gift from me to him, and I couldn't wait to see his face when he realized.

A lot had happened in the last three years.

River was about to become a big sister. Bryan and Carrie-Anne tied the knot at a gorgeous beach wedding last summer. Ezra was a starting wide receiver for the New York Giants, and Ashleigh spent her free time cheering on her fiancé from the stands. Gav and Pen had finally gotten their own place after she discovered she was ten weeks pregnant a few months ago. My sister and Aaron had beat us down the aisle in a small intimate ceremony last winter, and I had a sneaky suspicion they were trying to get pregnant. And Sofia and Cole had eventually retired Vera and rented a cute little place in Rixon East.

Life was good.

And it was about to get a whole lot better when I walked down the aisle toward my husband-to-be.

A knock at the door drew my attention and I glanced up just in time to see my dad poke his head inside. "Can I come in?"

"Of course."

"Jesus, Lily. You look... I think there's something in my eye."

"Dad." I blushed. "You don't look so bad yourself."

He looked dashing in his charcoal tux with sage cravat.

"I've waited a long time for this day," he said.

"I know. But we got here in the end."

"You did. And I'm so proud of you, sweetheart. Both of you."

"Thanks, Dad."

"You ready to go get your guy?" He crooked his arm, and I nodded, unable to hide my smile.

"So ready."

JASON

I'd already walked one daughter down the aisle, so I really should have been prepared for the torrent of emotions I felt as I guided Lily into position, awaiting our cue from the wedding coordinator.

The vast room was full of family and friends, new and old alike. I'd always pictured Lily having a small wedding. But when Kaiden's football career took off, their lives changed forever. And I was so fucking proud of my girl for embracing her life as the fiancée of one of the NFL's hottest players of the moment.

The success didn't go to Kaiden's head. He was still Kaiden. Still the guy head over heels in love with my daughter. A guy who would move mountains to make her happy.

He was all I could have asked for in a partner for Lily and more, and I didn't have a single reservation about giving her away to him today.

"Congratulations by the way," I said quietly as we waited.

Lily stared at me with utter surprise. "H-how did you know? I haven't told anyone yet."

"Because I know you, sweetheart. And you keep touching your stomach every few minutes. Your mom used to do that when she was pregnant with you."

"Oh. Kaiden... he doesn't know yet."

"My lips are sealed."

"You don't think it's too soon?"

"Am I internally freaking out that you're about to make me a grandpa, hell yes. But I'm so fucking happy for you, Lily. You're going to make a wonderful mom."

"Dad..." Her eyes welled. "Oh no, I can't cry. My makeup."

"You look beautiful, sweetheart. And I want you to know that there has been no greater single achievement in my life than watching you and Poppy grow and become the women you are today."

"Dad!"

"Sorry, sweetheart." I chuckled, struggling to keep my emotions in check. "But I needed you to know that."

There weren't many things that brought me to my knees, but my wife and two daughters were my kryptonite. My entire reason for breathing. And I would never take that for granted.

"You know, a wise man once told me you only needed to follow three rules for a happy life. Play hard. Fight hard. Love hard."

"He did, huh. Sounds like a smart man."

"The smartest." She grinned. "I love you, Dad."

"I love you too, sweetheart." I folded her hand in mine, my heart so full of love and pride. "Now let's go get you married."

The End.

AUTHOR'S NOTE

I have been writing in this world for over four years and it feels bittersweet to say goodbye to the series that quite literally changed my life.

The love for the Rixon Raiders (both OG and next gen) has been nothing short of beyond my wildest dreams.

Thank you for loving these characters, these stories, and this world.

I'm sure you'll see more of them in the future.

But for now, play hard... fight hard... and love hard.

Raiders forever!
L A xo

ABOUT THE AUTHOR

Reckless Love. Wild Hearts.

USA Today and *Wall Street Journal* bestselling author of over forty mature young adult and new adult novels, L. A. is happiest writing the kind of books she loves to read: addictive stories full of teenage angst, tension, twists and turns.

Home is a small town in the middle of England where she currently juggles being a full-time writer with being a mother/referee to two little people. In her spare time (and when she's not camped out in front of the laptop) you'll most likely find L. A. immersed in a book, escaping the chaos that is life.

L. A. loves connecting with readers.

The best places to find her are:
www.lacotton.com

Printed in Great Britain
by Amazon